AND A WOMAN SHALL LEAD THEM...

As the Hovertanks charged, the aliens led by the red Bioroid swooped at Veritechs who stood their ground, firing, in Battloid configuration. The red Bioroid fired quick, accurate bursts with the gun mounted on the Hovercraft and blew away two of the VTs, easily avoiding most of their fire and shrugging off the rest.

"Switch to Gladiator mode!" Dana called over the tac net. In midair the tanks shifted, reconfigured, *mechamorphosed.* When they landed, they were squat, two-legged, waddling gun turrets the size of a house, each with a massive primary-battery cannon stretching before it.

Dana took a deep breath and hopped her Gladiator high, landing to one end of the Bioroid firing line, to set up an enfilade. But an alien had spotted her, and swung to fire. Dana got off the first round and holed the outworld mecha with a searing energy bolt that left glowing, molten armor around the edges of the points of entry and departure.

"Gotcha!"

The ROBOTECH™ Series
Published by Ballantine Books:

ROBOTECH™ #7:

SOUTHERN CROSS

Jack McKinney

A Del Rey Book

BALLANTINE BOOKS • NEW YORK

CHAPTER

ONE

Those who were surprised at Dana Sterling's choice of a career in the military displayed not only a lack of understanding about Dana but also a failure to comprehend the nature of Protoculture, and how it shaped destiny.

After all, as a mere babe in arms Dana had played a pivotal part in a vital battle in the First Robotech War, the attack to take the Zentraedi's orbital mecha factory; with two of the greatest fighters in history as parents, is it any surprise that she would follow the warrior's trade?

But more important, Dana is the only offspring of a Human/Zentraedi mating on Earth, and the Protoculture was working strongly through her. She is to be a centerpiece of the ongoing conflict the Protoculture has shaped, and that means being a Robotech soldier in excelsis.

Dr. Lazlo Zand, notes for *Event Horizon: Perspectives on Dana Sterling and the Second Robotech War*

IT WAS A DATE THAT EVERY SCHOOLCHILD KNEW, though for some its significance had become a bit blurred.

But not for the people gathered in the auditorium at the Southern Cross Military Academy. Many of the veterans on the speakers' platform and among the academy teaching staff and cadre knew the meaning of the date because they had lived through it. Everyone in the graduating class revered it and the tradition of self-sacrifice and courage it represented—a tradition being passed along to them today.

"Today we celebrate not only your achievements as the

1

first graduating class of the Academy," Supreme Commander Leonard was saying, glowering down at the young men and women seated in rows before him. "We also celebrate the memory of the brave people who have served in our planet's defense before you."

Leonard continued, summarizing the last great clash of the Robotech War. If he had stopped in mid-syllable, pointed at any one of the graduating cadets, and asked him or her to take the story from there, the graduate would have done it with even more detail and accuracy.

They all knew it by heart: how Admiral Henry Gloval had taken the rusting, all-but-decommissioned SDF-1 into the air for a final confrontation with the psychopathic Zentraedi warlord Khyron, and died in the inferno of that battle.

They also knew the high honor roll of the women of the bridge watch who had died with him: Kim Young; Sammie Porter; Vanessa Leeds—all enlisted rating techs scarcely older than any of the cadets—and Commander Claudia Grant.

Sitting at the end of her squad's row, Cadet Major Dana Sterling looked down the line of faces beside her. One, with skin the color of dark honey, stared up into the light from the stage. Dana could see that Bowie Grant—nephew of that same Commander Claudia Grant and Dana's close friend since childhood—betrayed no emotion.

Dana didn't know whether to be content or worried. Carrying the name of a certified UEG hero could be a tough burden to bear, as Dana well knew.

Leonard went on about unselfish acts of heroism and passing the torch to a roomful of cadets, none of whom had yet reached twenty. They had had it all drilled into them for years, and were squirming in their seats, eager to get moving, to get to their first real assignments.

Or at any rate, *most* felt that way; looking down the line, Dana could see a withdrawn look on Bowie's face.

Leonard, with his bullet-shaped shaved head, massive as a bear and dripping with medals and ribbons, droned on to the end without saying anything new. It was almost silly for him to tell them that the Earth, slowly rebuilding in the seventeen years since the end of the Robotech War —fifteen since Khyron the Backstabber had launched his suicide attack—was a regrettably feudal place. Who would know that better than the young people who had grown up in it?

Or that there must be a devotion to the common good and a commitment to a brighter Human future? Who had more commitment than the young men and women sitting there, who had sworn to serve that cause and proved their determination by enduring years of merciless testing and training?

At last, thankfully, Leonard was done, and it was time to be sworn in. Dana came to attention with her squad, a unit that had started out company-size three years before.

Dana stood straight and proud, a young woman with a globe of swirling blond hair, average height for a female cadet, curvaceous in a long-legged way. She was blue-eyed, freckled, and pug-nosed, and very tired of being called "cute." Fixed in the yellow mane over her left ear was a fashion accessory appropriate to her time—a hair stay shaped to look like a curve of instrumentation suggesting a half-headset, like a crescent of Robotechnology sculpted from polished onyx.

The first graduating class received their assignments as they went up to the stage to accept their diplomas. Dana found herself holding her breath, hoping, hoping.

Then the supreme commander was before her, an overly beefy man whose neck spilled out in rolls above his tight collar. He had flaring brows and a hand that engulfed hers. But despite what the UEG public relations people said about him, she found herself disliking him. Leonard talked a good fight but had very little real combat experience; he was better at political wheeling and dealing.

Dana was trying to hide her quick, shallow breathing as she went from Leonard's too-moist handshake to the aide whose duty it was to tell the new graduates their first assignments.

The aide frowned at a computer printout. Then he glanced down his nose at Dana, looking her over disapprovingly. "Congratulations. You go to the Fifteenth squad, Alpha Tactical Armored Corps," he said with a sniff.

Dana had learned how to hide emotions and reactions at the academy; she was an old hand at it. So she didn't squeal with delight or throw her diploma into the air in exultation.

She was in a daze as she filed back to her seat, her squad following behind. The ATACs! The 15th squad! *Hovertanks!*

Let others try for the soft, safe, rear-echelon jobs, or the glamorous fighter outfits; nowadays the armored units were the cutting edge of Robotechnology, and the teeth and claws of the United Earth Government's military— the Army of the Southern Cross.

And the 15th had the reputation of being one of the best, if not *the* best. Under their daredevil leader, First Lieutenant Sean Phillips, they had become not only one of the most decorated but also one of the most court-martial-prone outfits around—a real black-sheep squad.

Dana figured that was right up her alley. She would have been graduating at the top of her class, with marks and honors succeeding generations would have found hard to beat, if not for certain peccadillos, disciplinary lapses, and scrapes with the MPs. She knew most of it wasn't really her fault, though. The way some people saw it, she had entered the Academy with several strikes against her, and she had had to fight against that the whole way.

Cadets who called her "halfbreed" usually found themselves flat on their faces, bleeding, with Dana kneeling on them. Instructors or cadre who treated her like just one more trainee found that they had a bright if impulsive pupil; those who gave any hint of contempt for her parentage found that their rank and station were no protection.

Cadet officers awakened to find themselves hoisted from flagpoles . . . a cadre sergeant's quarters were mysteriously walled in, sealing him inside. . . . The debutante cotillion of the daughter of a certain colonel was enlivened by a visit from a dozen or so chimps, baboons, and orangutans from the academy's Primate Research Center . . . and so on.

Dana reckoned she would fit into the 15th just fine.

She realized with a start that she didn't know where Bowie was going. She felt a bit ashamed that she had reveled in her own good fortune and had forgotten about him.

But when she turned, Bowie was looking up the row at her. He flashed his handsome smile, but there was a resigned look to it. He held his hand up to flash five outspread fingers—once, twice, three times.

Dana caught her breath. *He's pulled assignment to the 15th, too!*

Bowie didn't seem to be too elated about it, though. He closed the other fingers of his hand and drew his forefinger across his throat in a silent gesture of doom, watching her sadly.

The rest of the ceremonies seemed to go on forever, but at last the graduates were dismissed for a few brief days of leave before reporting to their new units.

Somehow Dana lost Bowie in the crush of people. He had no family or friends among the watching crowd; but neither did she. All the blood relatives they had were years-gone on the SDF-3's all-important mission to seek out the Robotech Masters somewhere in the far reaches of the galaxy.

The only adult to whom Dana and Bowie were close, Major General Rolf Emerson, was conducting an inspection of the orbital defense forces and unable to attend the ceremony. For a time in her childhood, Dana had had three very strange but dear self-appointed godfathers, but they had passed away.

Dana felt a spasm of envy for the ex-cadets who were surrounded by parents and siblings and neighbors. Then she shrugged it off, irritated at herself for the moment's self-pity; Bowie was all the family she had now. She went off to find him.

Even after three years in the Academy, Bowie was a cadet private, something he considered a kind of personal mark of pride.

Even so, as an upperclassman he had spacious quarters to himself; there was no shortage of space in the barracks, the size of the class having shrunk drastically since induction day. Of the more than twelve hundred young people who had started in Bowie's class, fewer than two hundred remained. The rest had either flunked out completely and gone home, or turned in an unsatisfactory performance and been reassigned outside the Academy.

Many of the latter had been sent either to regional militias, or "retroed" to assorted support and rear-echelon jobs. Others had become part of the colossal effort to rebuild and revivify the war-ravaged Earth, a struggle that had lasted for a decade and a half and would no doubt continue for years to come.

But beginning with today's class, Academy graduates would begin filling the ranks of the Cosmic Units, Tactical Air Force, Alpha Tactical Armored Corps, and the other components of the Southern Cross. Enrollment would be expanded, and eventually all officers and many of the enlisted and NCO ranks would be people who had attended the Academy or another like it.

Robotechnology, especially the second-generation brand currently being phased into use, required intense training and practice on the part of human operator-warriors. It was another era in human history when the citizen-soldier had to take a back seat to the professional.

And somehow Bowie—who had never wanted to be a soldier at all—was a member of this new military elite, entrusted with the responsibility of serving and guarding humanity.

Only, I'd be a lot happier playing piano and singing for my supper in some little dive!

Sunk in despair, Bowie found that even his treasured Minmei records couldn't lift his spirits. Hearing her sing "We Will Win" wasn't much help to a young man who didn't want anything to do with battle.

How can I possibly live this life they're forcing on me?

He plucked halfheartedly at his guitar once or twice, but it was no use. He stared out the window at the parade ground, remembering how many disagreeable hours he had spent out there, when the door signal toned. He turned the sound system down, slouched over, and hit the door release.

Dana stood there in a parody of a glamour pose, up on the balls of her feet with her hands clasped together behind her blond puffball hairdo. She batted her lashes at him.

"Well, it's about time, Bowie. How ya doing?" She walked past him into his room, hands still behind her head.

He grunted, adding, "Fine," and closed the door.

She laughed as she stood looking out at the parade ground. "Su-ure! Private Grant, who d'you think you're kidding?"

"Okay! So I'm depressed!"

She turned and gave him a little inclination of the head to acknowledge his honesty. "Thank you! And *why* are you depressed?"

He slumped into a chair, his feet up on a table. "Graduation, I guess."

They both wore form-fitting white uniforms with black boots and black piping reminiscent of a riding outfit. But their cadet unit patches were gone, and Dana's torso harness—a crisscross, flare-shouldered affair of burnt-orange leather—carried only the insignia of her brevet rank, second lieutenant, and standard Southern Cross crests. Dark bands above their biceps supported big, dark military brassards that carried the Academy's device; those would soon be traded in for ATAC arm brassards.

Dana sat on the bed, ankles crossed, holding the guitar idly. "It's natural to feel a letdown, Bowie; I do too." She strummed a gentle chord.

"You're just saying that to make me feel better."

"It's the truth! Graduation Blues are as old as education." She struck another chord. "Don't feel like smiling? Maybe I should sing for you?"

"No!" Dana's playing was passable, but her voice just wasn't right for singing.

He had blurted it out so fast that they both laughed. "Maybe I should tell you a story," she said. "But then, you know all my stories, Bowie." *And all the secrets I've ever been able to tell a full-breed Human.*

He nodded; he knew. Most people on Earth knew at least something of Dana's origins—the only known offspring of a Zentraedi/Human mating. Then her parents had gone, as his had, on the SDF-3 expedition.

Bowie smiled at Dana and she smiled back. They were two eighteen-year-olds about to take up the trade of war.

"Bowie," she said gently, "there's more to military life than just maneuvers. You can *make* it more. I'll help you;

you'll see!" She sometimes thought secretly that Bowie must wish he had inherited the great size and strength of his father, Vince Grant, rather than the compact grace and good looks of his mother, Jean. Bowie was slightly shorter than Dana, though he was fierce when he had to be.

He let out a long breath, then met her gaze and nodded slowly. Just then the alert whoopers began sounding.

It sent a cold chill through them both. They knew that not even a martinet like Supreme Commander Leonard would pick this afternoon for a practice drill. The UEG had too much riding on the occasion to end it so abruptly.

But the alternative—it was so grim that Dana didn't even want to think about it. Still, she and Bowie were sworn members of the armed forces, and the call to battle had been sounded.

Dana looked at Bowie; his face registered his dismay. "Red alert! That's us, Bowie! C'mon, follow me!"

He had been through so many drills and practices over the years that it was second nature to him. They dashed for the door, knowing exactly where they must go, what they must do, and superlatively able to do it.

But now, for the first time, they felt a real, icy fear that was not for their own safety or an abstract like their performance in some test. Out in the corridor Dana and Bowie merged with other graduates dashing along. Duffel bags and B-4 bags were scattered around the various rooms they ran past, clothing and gear strewn everywhere; most of the graduates had been packing to go home for a while.

Dana and Bowie were sprinting along with a dozen other graduates, then fifty, then more than half of the class. Underclassmen and women streamed from other barracks, racing to their appointed places. Just like a drill.

But Dana could feel it, smell it in the air, and pick it up through her skin's receptors: there was suddenly something out there to be feared. The cadet days of pretend-war were over forever.

Suddenly, emphatically, Dana felt a deep fear as something she didn't understand stirred inside her. And without warning she understood exactly how Bowie felt.

The young Robotech fighters—none older than nineteen, some as young as sixteen—poured out of their barracks and formed up to do their duty.

CHAPTER
TWO

It seems an imprecise thought or ridiculously metaphysical question to some, I know, but I cannot help but wonder. If the Robotech Masters rid themselves of their emotions, where did those emotions go?

Would there not be some conservation-of-energy law that would keep such emotions from disappearing completely but would see them transmuted into something else? Were they all simply converted to the Masters' vast longing for power, hidden knowledge, Protoculture, immortality?

And is that the by-product of stepped-up intellect? For if so, the Universe has played us a dreadful joke.

Zeitgeist, *Insights: Alien Psychology and the Second Robotech War*

COLD LUNA SWUNG IN ITS AGES-OLD ORBIT. IT HAD witnessed cataclysms in epochs long gone; it had watched the seemingly impossible changes that had taken place on Earth through the long eons of their companionship.

In recent times the moon had been a major landmark in the war between Zentraedi and Human, and looked down upon the devastation of Earth, fifteen years ago.

It was into the moon's cold lee that Captain Henry Gloval attempted to spacefold the SDF-1 at the outset of the Robotech War. There was a grievous miscalculation (or the intercession of a higher, Protoculture-ordained plan, depending on whether or not one listened to the eccentric Dr. Emil Lang), and the battle fortress leapt between dimensions to end up stranded out near Pluto.

But Gloval's plan, using Luna as cover and sanctuary, was still a sound one. And today, others were proving its worth.

Six stupendous ships, five miles from end to end through their long axes, materialized soundlessly and serenely in the dawn. They were as strong and destructive and Robotechnologically well-equipped as the Masters could make them.

Still, they were wary. Earth had already provided a charnel house for mighty fleets; the Robotech Masters had no more Zentraedi lives to spend, and had no intention of risking their own.

The voice of one of the Robotech Masters echoed through the command ship. He was one of the triumvirate that commanded the expedition, that ruled the ships, the Clonemasters, soldier-androids, Scientist Triads, and the rest.

He had sprung from the humanlike inhabitants of the planet Tirol, creatures who were virtually Human in plasm and appearance. But the Robotech Master's words came tonelessly, expressionlessly, and without sound; he was in contact with the Protoculture, and so spoke with mind alone.

He sent his thoughts into the communications bond that linked his mind with those of the transformed overlords of his race, beings like him but even more elevated in their powers and intellect—the three Elders.

The disembodied words floated in the chilly metallic

passageways. *We are in place, Elders—behind the moon of our objective, the third planet. All monitoring and surveillance systems are fully operational. You will begin receiving our primary transignal immediately.*

The technical apparatus of the ships pulsed and flowed with light, and the power of Protoculture. Some parts suggested blood vessels or the maze of a highway system, where pure radiance of shifting colors traveled; others resembled upside-down pagodas, suspended in the air, made of blazing materials like nothing that had ever appeared in the Solar System before.

The enigmatic energies opened a way across the light-years, to a sphere like a blue sapphire fifteen feet across. It threw forth brilliance, the glare splashing off the ax-keen, hawk-nosed faces of the three Elders who sat, enthroned in a circle, staring up at it. From far across the galaxy the Elders reached out with their minds to survey the Robotech Masters' situation.

The Elders were of a type, fey and gaunt, dressed in regal robes but looking more like executioners. All three had bald or shaven pates, their straight, fine hair falling below their shoulders. Under their sharp cheekbones were scarlike creases of skin, suggestive of tribal marks, that emphasized the severity of those laser-eyed faces.

They studied the images and data sent to them by their servants, the Robotech Masters.

One of them, Nimuul, whose blue hair was stirred by the air currents, mindspoke. His disembodied voice was thick as syrup. *The first transignal is of the area where the highest readings of Protoactivity have been recorded. Preliminary inspection indicates that it is unguarded.*

That pleased the other Elders, but none of them

evinced any emotion; they were above that, purged of it long ago.

Hepsis, of the silver locks, cheek resting on his thin, long-fingered fist, forearm so slender that it appeared atrophied, watched the transignal images balefully. *Hmm. You mean those mounds of soil and rock?* His voice was little different from Nimuul's.

Yes.

The three were looking at the transignal scene of the massive artificial buttes that stood in the center of what had once been the rebuilt Macross City. Although they didn't know the history of that long climactic battle of the Robotech War, and didn't realize what they were studying; the transignal was showing them the final resting places of the SDF-1, the SDF-2, and the flagship of Khyron the Backstabber.

All three ships had been destroyed in those few minutes of Khyron's last, suicidal attack; all had been quickly buried and the city covered over and abandoned due to the intense radiation, the last place ever to bear the name Macross.

Nimuul explained, *Zor's ship is probably— Wait!*

But he didn't have to draw their attention to it; Hepsis and Fallagar, the third Elder, could see it for themselves. For the first time in a very long time, the Elders of the Robotech Master race felt a misgiving that chilled even *their* polar nerves.

Three night-black figures wavered in the enormous transignal globe, defying the best efforts of the Masters' flagship's equipment to bring them into focus. The entities on the screen looked like tall, sinister wraiths, caped and cloaked, high collars shadowing their faces—all dark save for the light that beamed from their slitted eyes.

Three, of course—as all things of the Protoculture were triad.

The area is guarded by a form of inorganic sentry, Nimuul observed. *Or it could be an Invid trap of some kind.*

Fallagar, his hair an ice-blue somewhere between his comrades' shades, gave mental voice to their misgivings. *Or it might be something else*, he pointed out. *Something to do with the thrice-damned Zor.*

The images of the wraiths faded, then came back a bit against a background of static as the transignal systemry struggled to maintain it. It seemed that the ghostly figures *knew* they were under observation—were toying with the Masters. The lamp-bright eyes seemed to be staring straight at the Elders.

Then the image was gone, and nothing the Scientist Triad or Clonemasters could do would bring the Protoculture specters back into view. White combers of light washed through the blue globe of the transignal imager again, showing nothing of use.

By a commonality of mind, the Elders did not mention—refused to recognize—this resistance to their will and their instrumentality. The guardian wraiths would be discussed and dealt with at the appropriate time.

What do you wish to view next, Elders? asked a deferential Clonemaster.

Nimuul was suddenly even more imperious, eager to shake off the daunting effects of the long-distance encounter with the wraiths. *Show us the life forms that protected this planet from our Zentraedi warriors and now hold sway over the Protoculture Matrix.*

Yes, Elder, the Clonemaster answered meekly.

Hepsis told the other two, *The Humans who obliter-ated our Zentraedi are no longer present, according to my surveillance readings, my Brothers. But their fellows seem ready to protect their planet with a similiar degree of cun-ning and skill.*

The transignal was showing them quick images of the UEG forces: Cosmic Unit orbital forts and Civil Defense mecha, ATAC fighting machines, and the rest.

One intercepted TV transmission was a slow pan past the members of the 15th squad, monitored from a South-ern Cross public information broadcast. The Elders saw Humans with a hard-trained, competent look to them, and something else...something to which the Elders hadn't given thought in a long, long time.

It was youth. The camera showed them face after face —the smirking impertinence of Corporal Louie Nichols; the massive strength of Sergeant Angelo Dante; the flam-boyance of their leader, the swashbuckling ladies' man, Lieutenant Sean Phillips.

The Elders looked at their enemies, and felt a certain misgiving even more unsettling than that of the wraiths' image.

The three rulers of the Robotech Masters, privy to many of the secrets of Protoculture, were long-lived— would be Eternal, if their plans came to fruition. And as a result of that, *they feared death*, feared it more than any-thing. The fear was controlled, suppressed, but it was greater than any child's fear of his worst nightmares, more than any dread that any mortal harbored.

But the young faces in the camera pan didn't show that fear, not as the Elders knew it. The young understand death far better than their elders will usually acknowledge, especially young people in the military who know their number could come up any time, any day. The faces of the 15th, though, told that its members were willing to accept that risk—that they had found values that made it worthwhile.

That was disturbing to the Elders. They had clones and others who would certainly die for them, but none who would do so of their own volition; such a concept had long since been ground mercilessly from their race.

There was once more that unspoken avoidance of unpleasant topics among the Elders. Nimuul tried to sound indifferent. *It is hard for me to believe that these life forms could offer any resistance to us. They are so young and lack combat experience.*

He and his fellows were purposely ignoring an unpleasant part of the equation. If, in war, you're not willing to die for your cause but your enemy is willing to die for his, a terrible weight has been set on one side of the scales.

The Elders shuddered, each within himself, revealing nothing to one another. *I've seen enough of this*, Fallagar said, gathering his cloak like a falcon preparing to take wing, letting impatience show.

What images would you view now, Elders? asked the unseen Clonemaster tentatively.

Fallagar's silent voice resounded through the viewing chamber. *I think we have enough information on* these *life forms, so transmit whatever else you have on line. No matter how interesting these abstractions may be, the time has come for us to deal with the problems at hand!*

The globe swirled with cinnamon-red, came back to

blue, and showed the headquarters of the Army of the Southern Cross.

It was a soaring white megacomplex in the midst of Monument City. The countryside was marked with the corroded, crumpled miles-long remains of Zentraedi battlecruisers. They were rammed bow-first into the terrain, remnants of the last, long-ago battle.

The headquarters' central tower cluster had been built to suggest the white gonfalons, or ensigns, of a holy crusade hanging from high crosspieces. The towers were crowned with crenels and merlons, like a medieval battlement.

It all looked as if some army of giants had been marshaled. The architecture was meant to do just that—announce to the planet and the world the ideals and esprit of the Army of the Southern Cross.

The name "Southern Cross" was a heritage of those first days after the terrible Zentraedi holocaust that had all but eliminated Human life on Earth. Less damage had been done in the southern hemisphere than in the northern; many refugees and survivors were relocated there. A cohesive fighting force was quickly organized, its member city-states all lying within view of the namesake constellation.

Yes; we are through studying this planet for now, Fallagar declared. *Now establish contact with our Robotech Masters.* It was time for decisions to be passed down, from Elder to Robotech Master, and so on down the line at last to the Bioroid pilots who would once more carry death and fire to Earth in their war mecha.

Signals sprang among the six ships' communications

spars, which looked for all the world like huge, segmented insect legs.

What you have shown us has pleased us, Fallagar said with no hint of pleasure in his tone. *But now we must communicate with the inhabitants of this planet directly.*

While the Robotech Masters were being alerted to hear their overlords' word, blue-haired Nimuul said to his fellows, *I would make a point: these invisible entities who guard the Protoculture masses within the mounds on Earth may require special and unprecedented—*

Another voice came as the globe showed the gathered Robotech Masters. *Elders! We hear and serve you, and acknowledge your leadership and wisdom!*

Younger and at an earlier stage of their Protoculture-generated personal evolution, the Robotech Masters looked in every way like slightly less aged versions of the Elders. The Masters had the gleaming pates, the chevronlike skin seams under each cheekbone, the fine, straight hair that reached far down their backs and down their cheeks in long, wide sideburns. Their mental voices had been given that eerie vibrato by direct exposure to Protoculture. They wore monkish robes with sash belts, their collars in the shape of a blooming Invid Flower of Life.

Like virtually everyone in their culture, the Robotech Masters were a triumvirate. The slight differentiations among members of a triad, even differences of gender, served only to emphasize their oneness.

The Masters stood each upon a small platform, in a circle around their control monitor, an apparatus resembling a mottled technological mushroom five feet across, floating some five yards above the deck. It was the Proto-culture cap, source of their power.

Nimuul held his perpetual scowl. *Your transignal images were sufficiently informative, and you have reported that your war mecha are prepared. But now we must know if you are ready for us to join you.*

Fifteen years before, the race that called itself the Robotech Masters had sensed the enormous discharge of Protoculture energy in the last battle on Earth. But their instrumentality was depleted because the rebellious genius Zor had sent the last Protoculture Matrix away in the SDF-1, and the Zentraedi's destruction and the endless war against the Invid had made great demands on the remaining reservoirs.

The Masters lacked the Protoculture power to send their armada to the target world by the almost instantaneous shortcut of hyperspace-fold generation. Therefore, the Elders had dispatched the six enormous mother ships, with their complements of assault craft and Bioroids, on a fifteen-year voyage by more conventional superluminal drive. Now that the journey was over, the Elders meant to rejoin the expedition by means of a small spacefold transference—of themselves.

But Shaizan, who most often spoke for the Robotech Masters, answered, his blue-gray hair flowing with the movements of his head. *No, Elders! We are very close to regaining the lost Protoculture masses and recovering secrets that Zor attempted to take to the grave with him. But we must not make the same mistakes the Zentraedi made!*

We must know more about their strengths and weaknesses, added Dag, another Master, gazing up at the Elders' image.

Nimuul's frown deepened. *You must not fail.* The Robotech Masters all bowed deeply to their *own* Masters, the Elders.

When the Elders broke contact, the Robotech Masters looked in turn to the Clonemasters and the other triumvirates gathered below the hovering Protoculture cap. Shaizan, gathering his blue robes about him, his collar hanging like an orange flower around his neck, snapped, "Now, do you understand the plan, and do you anticipate any problems, group leader?

The Clonemasters and the rest looked in every way like Human males and females, fair-skinned for the most part. They tended toward an aesthete slimness, with long hair and form-fitting clothing that might have come from the early renaissance, draped with short capelets and cloaks. Among their triumvirates there was little differentiation in appearance or clothing.

The Clonemaster group leader replied in a voice somewhere between that of a Human and that of a Robotech Master. "Master, every Bioroid pilot is briefed and prepared to execute the first phase exactly as you have decreed. The only problem is in keeping our operators functional; our Protoculture supplies are quite minimal."

Shaizan frowned at the group leader as the Elders had frowned upon the Robotech Masters, with that same angry ruthlessness. "Then double the numbers of Bioroid fighting mecha assigned to the attack. You may draw additional Protoculture from the ships' engines only if it proves absolutely indispensable to success of the mission."

Dag, more lantern-jawed than his triumvirate-siblings,

the most intellectual of them, added, "If possible, I would like some Human captives for experimental purposes."

Bowkaz, the most military of the three Robotech Masters, contradicted, as was his prerogative in tactical matters. "No," he told Dag. To the group leader, he added, "You will proceed, but only as per our original orders. Understood?"

The group leader inclined his head respectfully. "As you will."

Shaizan nodded, inspecting the Clonemasters and the other triumvirates coldly. "Then we look forward to your success and trust that you will not fail."

The group leader said emotionlessly, "We understand the consequences of failure, Master."

As did everyone on the expedition, the Robotech Masters' last desperate throw of the dice. The group leader met their scowls. The Bioroid war machines were waiting to bring destruction to the unsuspecting Humans.

"We will not fail you," he vowed.

When the clone triumvirates had hurried away to execute the probing attack, the Robotech Masters summoned up an image of the maze of systemry in their flagship. The living Protoculture instrumentality suggested internal organs, vascular tubes, clear protoplasmic tracts strobing with the ebb and flow of energy.

Dag bespoke his fellows. "If we could capture a Human, our mindprobe would reveal whether they've discovered any hint of the existence of the Protoculture Matrix."

"Not necessarily," Bowkaz replied.

They all looked at the shrunken mass of Protoculture

left to them. The secret of making a Matrix had died with Zor, and there was no other source of Protoculture in the known universe. This Matrix was the Robotech Masters' last chance for survival.

"There will be time to interrogate the Humans once they lie defeated and helpless beneath our heel," Shaizan said.

CHAPTER
THREE

*I couldn't really tell you who said it first—commo op,
Black Lion, cruiser crewmember—but* somebody *did, and,
given the circumstances, everybody just naturally picked it up,
starting then and there: the Second Robotech War.*

Lieutenant Marie Crystal, as quoted in "Overlords,"
History of the Robotech Wars, Vol. CXII

SPACE STATION LIBERTY SWUNG SLOWLY IN ITS
Lagrange Five holding place, out near Luna. It combined
the functions of outpost fortress, communications nerve
center, and way station along the routes to Earth's distant
colonies on the moon and elsewhere. Its complex commo
apparatus, apparatus that wouldn't function as well on
Earth, was the Human race's only method of maintaining
even intermittent contact with the SDF-3 expedition. Liberty was in many ways the keystone to Earth's defenses.

And so it was the natural target.

"Liberty, this is Moon Base, Moon Base!"

The Moon Base communications operator adjusted the
gain on his transmitter desperately, taking a moment to
eye the radar paints he had punched up on a nearby display screen.

Five bogies, big ones, had come zooming around from

the moon's dark side. The G2 section was already sure they were nothing the Human race had even used or seen before. Performance and power readings indicated that they were formidable vessels, and course projections had them headed straight for Liberty, at appalling speed.

"Why won't they answer? WHY?" The commo op fretted, but some sort of interference had been jamming everything since the bogies first appeared. And nothing Moon Base could get off the ground could possibly catch the UFOs.

The op felt a cold sweat on his brow, for himself as well as for the unsuspecting people aboard the space station. If Liberty were knocked out, that would leave Moon Base and the other scattered Human sentry posts in the Solar System cut off, ripe for casual eradication.

The indicators on his instruments suddenly waffled; either the enemy had been obliged to channel power away from jamming and into weapons, shields, or whatever, or the signal-warfare countermeasures computers had come up with a way to punch through a transmission. A dim, static-fuzzed voice from Liberty acknowledged.

The Moon Base op opened his headset mike and began sending with frantic haste.

"Space Station Liberty, this is Moon Base. Flash message, I say again, flash message! Five bogies closing on you at vector eight-one-three-slash-four-four-niner! You may not have them on your scopes; they have been fading in and out on ours. We didn't know they were here until we got a visual. Possible hostiles, I say again, possible hostiles. They're coming straight for you!"

In the Liberty Station commo center, another op was signaling the duty officer that a flash message—a priority emergency—was incoming, even as he recorded the Moon Base transmission.

When it was done, he turned and exercised a prerogative put in place during the rebuilding of Earth after the Zentraedi holocaust. There wasn't time for an officer to get to the commo center, evaluate the message, get in touch with the G3 staff, and have a red alert declared. Every second was critical; the Human race had learned that the hard way.

No op had ever used it before, but no op had ever faced this situation before. With the decisive slap of a big, illuminated red button, a commo center corporal put the space station on war footing, and warned Earth to follow suit.

He tried to piece together the rest of what the Moon Base op was saying just as he spied a watch officer headed his way. The op covered his mike with his hand and called out, "Red flag, ma'am! Tell 'em to get the gun batteries warmed up, 'cause we're in trouble!"

The commo lieutenant nodded. She turned at once to a secure intercom, signaling the station's command center. Klaxons and alarm hooters began their din.

"*Battle stations, battle stations! Laser and plasma gunners, prepare to open fire!*"

Armored gunners dashed to their posts as Liberty went on full alert. The heavily shielded turrets opened and the ugly, gleaming snouts of the twin- and quad-barreled batteries rose into view, traversing and coming to bear on the targets' last known approach vector.

Near the satellite fortress, a flight of patrol ships swung around to intersect the bogies' approach. They were big, slow, delta-shaped cruisers, slated for replacement in the near future. They were the first to feel the power of the Robotech Masters.

The five Robotech Master assault ships came, sand-red and shaped like flattened bottles. The leader arrowed in at the Earth craft, opening up with energy cannon. A white-hot bolt opened the side of the cruiser as if gutting a fish. Atmosphere and fireballs rushed from the Human ship. Within it, crewmen and -women screamed, but only briefly.

The Masters' warcraft plunged in, eager for more kills.

"I can't raise any of the patrol cruisers, ma'am," the Liberty Station commo op told TASC Lieutenant Marie Crystal. "And three of them have disappeared from the radar screens."

Marie looked up at the commo link that had been patched through to her by the commander of the patrol flotilla with which her Tactical Armored Space Corps fighter squadron was serving. She nodded, her delicate jaw set.

She was a pale young woman in battle armor, with blue eyes that had an exotic obliqueness to them, and short, unruly hair like black straw. There was an intensity to her very much like that of an unhooded bird of prey.

"Roger that, Liberty Station. Black Lions will respond." She ran a fast calculation; the flotilla had diverted from its usual near-Earth duties when the commo breakdown occurred, and was now very close to Liberty —close enough for binocular and telescope sighting on the explosions and energy-bolt signatures out where the sneak attack had taken place, beyond the satellite.

"Our ETA at your position in approximately ninety

seconds from launch." He acknowledged, white-faced and sweating, and Marie broke the patch-up. Then she signaled her TASC unit, the Black Lions, for a hot scramble.

"Attention all pilots. Condition red, condition red. This is not a drill, I say again, this is not a drill. Prepare for immediate launch, all catapults. Black Lions prepare to launch."

The decks reverberated with the impact of running armored boots. Marie led the way to the hangar deck, her horned flight helmet in one hand. There was all the usual madness of a scramble, and more, because no one among the young Southern Cross soldiers had ever been in combat before.

Marie boarded her Veritech fighter with practiced ease, even though she was weighted down by her body armor. The scaled-up cockpit had room for her in the bulky superalloy suit, but even so, and even after years of practice she found it a bit more snug than she would have liked.

The Tactical Armored Space Corps' front-line fighter-craft had been decreased in size quite a bit since the Rototech War because they no longer needed to go to a Battloid-mode size that would let them slug it out toe-to-toe with fifty-foot-tall Zentraedi warriors or their huge Battlepods.

Her maint crew got her seated properly and ready to taxi for launch. As Marie sat studying the gauges and instruments and indicators on her panel, she didn't realize how much like a slim, keen-eyed Joan of Arc she looked in her armor.

Strange, she brooded. *It's not like I thought it would be. I'm anxious but not nervous.*

Crewpeople with spacesuits color-coded to their jobs raced around, seeing to ordnance and moving craft, or racing to take their places in the catapult crews. They, too, tended to be young, a part of Robotechnology's new generation, shouldering responsibilities and facing hazards that made them adults while most of them were still in their teens. Even in peacetime, death was a part of virtually every cruise, and the smallest mishap could cost lives.

The Black Lions launched and formed up; the enemy ships turned toward them but altered course at the last moment, launching their own smaller craft.

"What *are* those things?" Second Lieutenant Snyder, whose callsign was Black Beauty, yelled when the enemy fighters came into visual range, already firing.

Gone were the simple numeral callsigns of a generation before; Earth was a feudal hegemony of city-states and regional power structures, bound by virtually medieval loyalties, under the iron fist of the UEG, and the planet's military reflected that. So did the armor of the Southern Cross's ultratech knights, including Marie's own helmet, with its stylized horns.

"Shut up and take 'em!" Marie snapped; she hated unnecessary chatter on a tac net. "And stick with your wingmen!"

But she didn't blame Black Beauty for being shocked. *So, the Zentraedi are back*, she thought. *Or somebody a lot like them.*

The bogies that were zooming in at the Black Lions were faceless armored figures nearly the size of the alien invaders who appeared in 1999 to savage Earth and initiate the Robotech War. These were different, though: They were Humanoid-looking, though insectlike; Zentraedi Battlepods were like headless alloy ostriches bristling with cannon.

Moreover, these things rode swift, maneuverable saucer-shaped Hovercraft, like outlandish walking battleships riding waterjet platforms.

But they were fast and deadly, whatever they were. The Hovercraft dipped and changed vector, prodigal with their power, performing maneuvers that seemed impossible outside of atmosphere. Up until today that had always been a Veritech specialty.

About twenty of the intruders dove in at a dozen Black Lions, and the dogfighting began. Fifteen years had gone by since the last time Human and alien had clashed, and the answered prayers that were peace were suddenly vacated.

And the dying hadn't changed.

The small volume of space, just an abstract set of coordinates, became the new killing ground. VT and Bioroid circled and pounced at one another, fired or dodged depending upon who had the advantage, maneuvered furiously, and came back for more.

The aliens fired extremely powerful energy weapons, most often from the bulky systems packages that sat before them on their control stems. That gave the Lions the eerie feeling that a horde of giant metallic water-skiers was trying to immolate them.

But the arrangement only *looked* funny; incandescent rays flashed from the control-stem projectors, and three TASC fliers died almost at once. The saucer-shaped-

Hoverplatforms turned to seek new prey. This time they demonstrated that they could fire from apertures in the bodies of their saucercraft as well as those in the control-stem housings.

"Black Beauty, Black Beauty, two bogies on your tail!" John Zalenga, who was known as White Knight, called out the warning. "Go to turbo-thrust!" Marie spared a quick glance to her commo display, and saw Zalenga's white-visaged helmet with its brow-vanes on one side of a split-screen, Snyder's ebony headgear, like some turbaned, veiled muslim champion's on the other.

But before Snyder could do anything about his dilemma, the two were on him, their fire crisscrossing on his VT's tail. Marie heard the fight rather than saw it, because at that moment she had the shot she wanted at a darting alien Hovercraft.

VT armament had changed in a generation: gone were the autocannon and their depleted transuranic shells. Amplified laser arrays sent pulses of destructive power through the vacuum. Armored saucer-platform and armored alien rider disappeared in a cloud of flame and shrapnel.

Marie's gaze was level and intent behind her tinted visor. "We lost Black Beauty; the rest of you start flying the way you were taught! Start flying like Black Lions!"

Outside of a few minor brushfire conflicts over borders, the VTs of Marie's generation had never flown combat before. Certainly, Aerial Combat School was nothing like this: real enemy fire and real friends being blown to rags of sizzling flesh and cinders, with the next volley coming at *you*.

But Marie's voice and their training put the Lions back

in control. The survivors got back into tight pairs, covering one another as the Bioroids came back for another run.

"Going to Guardian mode," Marie bit out, her breath rasping a little in her helmet facemask. They were all pulling lots of gees in the hysterical maneuvering of the dogfight; as trained, they locked their legs and tightened their midsections to keep the blood up in their heads, where it was needed. The grunting and snorting for breath made the Black Lions' tac net sound as if some desperate tug-of-war were in progress.

Marie pulled the triplet-levers as one; her VT began changing.

None of the intricacies of mechamorphosis mattered much to the young VT leader with a sky full of bogies coming at her. All Marie really cared about was that when she summoned up her craft's Guardian configuration, the order was obeyed.

She could feel the craft shifting and changing shape around her, modules sliding and structural parts reconforming themselves, like some fantastic mechanical origami. In moments, Veritech became Guardian, a giant figure like a cross between a warrior and a space-battlecruiser, a sleek eagle of Robotechnology.

"Got you covered, White Knight," she told Zalenga. "Here they come." The Masters' battle mecha surged in at them, the flashes of their fire lighting the expression-less insect eyes of the Bioroids' head-turrets.

But the next joust of spaceborne paladins was very different from what had gone before. The Guardian had most of the speed of a Veritech, but the increased maneuverability and firepower that came from bringing it closer to anthropomorphic form. More or less the form of the Bioroids.

But more, Marie Crystal *thought* her craft through its change and its actions. The secret of Robotech mecha lay in the pilot's helmet—the "thinking cap," as it had been dubbed. Receptors there picked up thought impulses and translated them into the mecha's actions. No other control system could have given a machine that kind of agility and battle-prowess, which seemed more like those of a living thing.

Marie dodged one Hovercraft's fire, neatly missing that of the thing's companion, darting like a superalloy dragonfly. She controlled her mecha with deft manipulations of the gross motor-controls—hand and foot controls there in the cockpit—but more important, she *thought* her Guardian through the firefight. Mental imaging was the key to Robotech warfare.

The lead Bioroid was firing at a place Marie's Guardian no longer occupied. She blasted it dead center with an almost frugally short burst of intense fire, a hyphen of novafire that was gone nearly before it had begun. The Bioroid erupted outward in fireball demise.

She ducked the backup Bioroid's cannonade, too, and wove through it to fix the alien mecha in her gunsight reticle and shoot. The second Bioroid was an articulated fortress—bulbous-forearmed, bulbous-legged—one moment, and a superheated gas cloud headed for entropy the next.

The other Black Lions weren't slow to pick up on the new tactics. Some went to Guardian mode, and one or two to Battloid—the Veritech equivalent of the Bioroids —while one or two remained in Fighter mode. The Bioroids simply could not adjust to the smorgasbord of Earthly war-mecha suddenly facing them.

Tables turned, and it was the invader mecha that disappeared in spheres of white-hot explosion. Then it became apparent that they had had enough; like oily, scuttling beetles, the two or three survivors hunkered over their control stems and fled.

A controller from the Lions' cruiser got through to them just as they were preparing to mechamorphose and pursue the enemy until none were left.

"Black Lion Team, break contact! All Veritechs, break contact! Let 'em go for now, Lions, and return to the ship at once."

The ballooning explosions began to die away; Marie gathered up her unit unhurriedly, enjoying mastery of the battlefield.

But she knew that the tactics that had won the Lions this day's fight might not be as effective next time. And she knew, too, that the force her team had faced was probably a negligible number in terms of the enemy's total strength.

She thrust the thought aside. Today was a victory; embattled humanity, cast into the eye of the storm of interstellar Robotech warfare again, had to relearn the skill of taking things one moment, one battle, one breath of life at a time.

CHAPTER
FOUR

It was Bowie I'd legally taken as my ward, his parents being among my closest friends, but it was often Dana who gave me greater cause for worry. With her mixed parentage and the grief she sometimes got about it, she was often torn between two distinct modes of behavior, the sternly military and the wildly anti-authoritarian

And, none of us really know what it was Lang, and later Zand, were doing to her in those experiments when she was a baby. We suspect it had something to do with Protoculture, and activating the alien side of her nature.

But Zand knows one thing: he knows how close I came to killing him with my bare hands that day when I came to take baby Dana away from him. And if anything ever happens to her because of what he did, Zand's fears will be borne out.

From the personal journal of Major General Rolf Emerson

LIKE MOST SOUTHERN CROSS MILITARY FACILITIES, the place was roomy. The devastating attacks of the Zentraedi had seen to it that Earth would have no problems with population density for some time to come.

This one was a large, truncated cone, an airy building of smoky blue glass and gleaming blue tile, set on a framework of blue-tinted alloy. The architecture had a nostalgic art-deco look to it. It was big even though it served only as barracks to a relatively few people; much of the above-ground area was filled with parts and equipment storage and repair areas, armory, kitchen and dining and lavatory facilities, and so on. In some ways it was a self-contained world.

Mounted on its front was an enormous enlargement of a unit crest, that of the Alpha Tactical Armored Corps, the ATACs, and beneath that the squad designation: 15.

The crest was lavish, almost rococo, with rampant lion and unicorn, crown, gryphon, stars, shields, and the rest. The viewer had to look closely to see that one element of what was supposed to be crossed machetes looked more like...rabbit ears. The 15th had an old, gallant, and highly decorated past but a reputation for trouble, and for deviltry as well. The origin of the rabbit ears in its heraldry had a hundred different versions, and quite possibly none of them were true.

Inside, in a unit ready-room, there was an unusual level of banter going on, with almost a celebratory air. The same alarm that had disrupted Dana's graduation day proceedings, as word came of attack from space, had taken the ATACs off a peacetime footing.

Dana and Bowie had spent a week with the 15th, getting ready for the follow-up attack that never came. But at least there was no more falling out for silly make-work details or drudge jobs from the duty roster; the 15th had made sure it was ready to go, then had been ordered to stand-to and remain in barracks pursuant to further orders.

In civilian terms, it was a little like a small lottery win. The troopers of the 15th were napping or reading or chatting amiably to one another or watching vid. Bowie Grant was fooling around at an ancient upright piano that someone had scavenged for the 15th over a decade before; by diligent work he had gotten it back in tune, and now played it with eyes closed. On his torso harness and arm brassards were the 15th's crests.

Near him, Louie Nichols listened indifferently to the music while he cleaned and reassembled a laser pistol. Totally synthesized synaptic-inductance music with enhanced simu-sensory effects was more to Louie's liking; the lanky corporal was a sort of maverick technical genius given to endless tinkering and preoccupation with gadgetry.

Still, Bowie's music wasn't too bad for primitech stuff, Louie decided. Bowie was liked well enough after a week in the 15th, but he was still a bit of an oddball, like Louie himself. A man who looked out at the world through big, square, heavily tinted goggles—few people had seen Louie's eyes, even in the shower. Louie had decided Bowie was a misfit and therefore somewhat of a kindred soul, and that Dana was a bit of the same. So he had taken to the 15th's newest troopers.

Others had accepted them too, though there was a little coolness toward Dana; she had been assigned as the 15th's new Executive Officer since the old XO had been hospitalized after a training maneuver injury. It was all perfectly ordinary, since she had been commissioned out of the Academy, but—she was the first woman in the 15th, one of the first in the ATAC.

Two privates were killing time with a chess game. "D'you hear the latest skinny?" the smaller one asked casually. "Our CO's gonna be in stockade for a while."

His big, beefy opponent shrugged, still studying his bishop's dilemma. "Too bad Sean's such a ladies' man— too bad for *him*."

"He shouldn't've made a pass at a superior officer," the first said.

A third, who had been kibbitzing, contributed, "Sean just didn't have his mind right, or he would've known better. Ya just *don't* go grabbing a colonel's daughter like that."

No, indeed; especially when the daughter was herself a captain. But scuttlebutt had it that the grabbing had gone rather well and that initial reaction was favorable, until the ATAC Officer of the Day wandered in and found army furniture being put to highly unauthorized use, as it were, by army personnel who were supposedly on duty. It was just about then that the colonel's daughter started yelling for help.

It was a brief court-martial, and word was that Lieutenant Sean Phillips grinned all through it. A constant stream of letters and CARE packages, sent by other female admirers, was brightening up his guardhouse stay.

Sergeant Angelo Dante, engrossed in a conversation of his own, snorted, "Aw, all she is is a snotty, know-it-all teenager!" He had served under Sean for some time, and resented seeing him replaced. He was so preoccupied with it that he didn't realize the rec-room door had slid open and the replacement was standing there.

"Why, Angelo, you say the sweetest things," a lively female voice said mockingly. Everyone looked around, startled, to see Dana posed glamorously in the doorway. The brevet pips were gone from her torso harness; she had been promoted from temporary XO—a kind of on-the-job training—to the CO slot, now that Sean was going to be spending some time playing rock-hockey over at the stockade.

Bowie stood up from the piano with a smile on his face. "Congratulations, Lieutenant Sterling," he said with genuine delight, much as he disliked the military.

Nobody bothered to call attention; the 15th was a casual kind of place under Sean. But there were a few appreciative whistles and murmurs for Dana's pose, and Evans, the supply sergeant, raised a coffee mug to her from his place on a stool at the (currently dry) bar. "A toast! To the cutest second lieutenant in the ATACs!" he said, pronouncing it *AY-tacks*.

Other voices seconded the sentiment. Dana strolled over toward Angelo Dante with a seductive, swivel-hipped gait. "What's the matter, Angie? Don't think I'm tough enough?" She gave him a languorous smile and kept it there as she gave him a swift kick in the shin.

Angelo was utterly shocked, but he barely let out a grunt; he was a tall, muscular man, well known for his strength and ability to withstand punishment. Dana let the guffaws and catcalls go on for a few seconds as the 15th razzed Angelo for being taken off guard. Angelo rubbed his shin and snarled at her retreating back, but inside he was suddenly reevaluating his opinion of "Miss Cadet," as he had been calling her.

Dana crossed to the window, then whirled on them, cutting through the hoots and catcalls. "Fall in! On the double!"

There was a confused half-second of disbelief, then the 15th scrambled to stand at attention in two precise ranks, facing her. "Now what's she trying to prove?" Angelo heard someone mutter.

Dana looked them over, hands locked behind her back. She waited a few seconds in the absolute silence, then said, "Y'know, I've been giving this a lot of thought. And I've decided that this squad is dull. Definitely cute, but dull."

She walked along the front rank, inspecting her new command. "However, I *think* there's still hope for you, so prepare to move out!"

She had come to the end of the front rank, where Angelo stood glowering at her. "Something on your mind, Angie?"

He said, tight-lipped, "I could be wrong about this, but aren't we on ready-reaction duty this week?"

The ready-reaction squad was a kind of fire brigade, ready to move at once should any trouble occur, either at the base or elsewhere. The fact that it had to be ready to move on a moment's notice meant that the ready-reaction force usually kept all personnel in or immediately around its barracks.

But Dana gave Angelo a scornful look. "What's that got to do with a training maneuver?"

It wouldn't actually be breaking a reg, but it would be bending some. "Well, we haven't gotten official clearance from regimental HQ."

If there was a funny, warm Human side to her, there was a fire-breathing Zentraedi amazon side, too. Dana's eyes narrowed and her nostrils flared. "If you're looking to be busted to buck private, Dante, just keep doing what you're doing! 'Cause *I* give the orders here and *you* obey them!"

The usually gruff Angelo unexpectedly broke into a smile. "If you say so, Lieutenant." The simplest solution would be to give the kid enough rope, and even egg her on a little without being too obvious about it.

Dana showed locked teeth and the assembled 15th wondered silently if steam was going to start coming out of her ears. "If you have a problem, *Sergeant*, maybe I ought to send you to get your Chaplain Card punched. Or do you just resent taking orders from a woman?"

That stung Angelo, who *was* what he liked to think of as a little old-fashioned, but didn't want to be branded a sexist. He drew a deep breath. "That's not it at all, Lieutenant, but with all this trouble out at Liberty and the Moon Base—what if something happens and we're not here?" He gave her a condescending smile.

Dana was furious. Dante plainly didn't think she was fit to command, to fill the shoes of the dashing, devil-may-care Sean Phillips. So the 15th respected officers with a wild streak only, officers who were daredevils? She'd show them that Dana Sterling could lead the pack!

"In that case, Sergeant," she said, smirking, "why don't *you* just sit here and twiddle your thumbs? The rest of you, get to your Hovercycles! Move out!"

She's acting like it's all just a big picnic, Angelo saw. *I just hope she doesn't get us* all *into trouble*.

But as the 15th dashed for the drop-rack, whooping and shouting, Angelo was right with them.

The drop-rack was a sort of skeletal ladder that, like a conveyor belt or pater-noster, moved downward end-lessly, a modern-day firemen's pole giving quick access to the motor pools below ground level.

At the first motor pool level, the troopers jumped from the drop-rack with practiced ease, just before it dis-appeared through a square opening in the floor, bound for the next level down, where the Hovertanks were kept.

The 15th dashed to its Hovercycles, one-seater sur-

face-effect vehicles built for speed and maneuverability.
Dana leapt astride her saddle, taking the handlebars.
"Recon patrol in G sector, gentlemen!"

She settled her goggles on her face, gunned the engine.
"Let's . . . go-ooo!" The 15th shot away after her, yahoo-
ing and giving rebel yells.

Dana laughed, exulting. *Whoever said a drill couldn't
be fun?*

First they barreled through Monument City on a joyride that sent civilian pedestrians scuttling for safety. The
cycles roared up and around access ramps and clover-
leafs, threaded through traffic, and got into cornering
duels with one another. The troopers yelled to one another and howled their encouragement to Dana, who had
taken the lead.

She loved it, loved setting the pace and hearing her
men cheer her on. "See if you can keep up with me,
guys!" She gave a burst of thruster power, leaping the
railing to land on an access ramp higher up and several
yards away. They were headed the wrong way, against
oncoming traffic.

Somehow, nobody was killed; the cycles deftly jumped
the cars with thruster bursts, and the careening civilian
cars managed not to annihilate one another as they
slewed to avoid the troopers. Fists were shaken at them,
and obscenities hurled, but the Southern Cross soldiers
were above it all, literally and figuratively.

Then it was down onto a major traffic artery, for a flat
speed run into the badlands on Monument City's outskirts. Rusting Zentraedi wreckage of the Robotech War
dotted the landscape. This particular area still hadn't re-

covered from the alien fusillade that had devastated nearly the entire planet some seventeen years before; it looked more like the moon.

"Fokker Base is only a few more miles," Dana yelled over the wind and the sound of the engines. "We'll stop there!"

As Bowie passed the word, she thought sarcastically, *All this commanding is* such *a lot of work*. Then she laughed aloud into the rushing air.

Marie Crystal and her Black Lions were relaxing in the squadron canteen when the shrilling of the Hovercycle engines approached. The VT pilots had just finished an afternoon of target runs.

Dana came to a stop with a blare of thruster power and a blast of dust and debris. She hopped from her cycle as the rest of the 15th drew up next to her. She looked the enormous base over; Fokker wasn't far from the Human-made mounds that covered the fallen SDF-1, SDF-2, and the flagship of Khyron the Backstabber.

The place was the home of Tactical Air Force and Cosmic Units along with the TASC Veritechs, as well as experimental facilities and an industrial complex. It was also a commo nexus and regional command headquarters.

Inside the canteen a mohawked VT pilot inspected the 15th through a large permaplas window. "Uh-oh, looks like school's out."

Dana was gazing back at the pilots now. "Hey, the eagles are being led by a dove, huh?" said one Lion approvingly.

Marie set hands on hips and *hmmph*ed. "More like turkeys being led by a goose," she sneered.

Dana led her men in and was confronted by First Lieutenant Marie Crystal. Dana saluted, and Marie barked, "State your mission."

Dana saw that the hospitality carpet was definitely not out. There had always been rivalry between the TASCs and the ATACs; their VTs and Hovertanks had some Robotech capabilities in common and therefore at times ended up with overlapping mission responsibilities. There was strong disagreement about which mecha was better in this mode or that, and which was the all-around superior. More than a few fists had flown over the subject.

This was the first time Dana had encountered such hostility, though. She had chosen Hovertanks because, she was certain, they were the most versatile, formidable mecha ever invented, so she wasn't about to take guff from some VT bus driver.

Dana identified herself, then drawled, "It's been a hard ride an' a dusty road. Y'wouldn't happen to have a little firewater around, would yuh, pard?"

That had the 15th guffawing and the Black Lions choking on their coffee. Marie Crystal's brows met. "What'd you do, kid, escape from a western? Don't you know how a commander's supposed to behave, even the commander of a flock of kiddie cars?"

Now Dana was annoyed, too. "My squad's got more citations for excellence than you could fit into your afterburner! Number one in every training maneuver and war game it's ever been in!"

Marie smiled indulgently, maddeningly. "Games don't prove a thing; only combat does."

Dana decided things had gone far enough. The 15th

and the Lions were eyeing one another, some of them rubbing their knuckles thoughtfully.

Dana turned to go, but threw back over her shoulder, "My unit would never turn its back on a *real* fight, Lieutenant."

Her troopers began to follow her, but one of the VT fliers—Eddie Muntz, a pinch-faced little guy with a reputation as a troublemaker—jumped to his feet. He called after them, "Hey, wait! Don'tcha want a cuppa coffee?"

Royce, a tall, skinny trooper wearing horn-rimmed glasses, turned to tell him no thanks. He got most of a full cup flung into his face.

Eddie Muntz stood laughing, managing to gasp, "Nothing like a good cuppa Java, I always say!" He was convulsing so hard that he didn't see what was headed his way.

"Try *this*," Bowie Grant invited, and tagged Muntz with an uppercut that sent him crashing back across the table. Bowie didn't like the army, or violence, but senseless cruelty was something that simply enraged him.

A couple of Lions helped Muntz to his feet, one of them growling, "So, the kids want to play rough."

Muntz wiped blood from his split lip. "Pretty good for somebody in day care," he admitted. Then he launched himself through the air to tackle Bowie.

But Bowie was ready for him; the ATAC trooper caught a hold of Muntz's uniform at the same time bringing up one foot and setting it in the juncture where leg met abdomen. Bowie fell backward to the floor, rolling, pulling his opponent with him, and pushing him with the foot that was in Muntz's midsection. It was just like Bowie had been taught at Academy hand-to-hand classes;

with a wild scream the practical joker went flying through the air straight over Bowie's head.

Bowie's only miscalculation was that Dana was right in Muntz's trajectory. The VT pilot crashed into her head-first and bore her to the floor. They lay in a tangle of arms and legs, with Dana hollering at the dazed Muntz to get off her.

Dana's scrabbling hand encountered a piece of metal, a table leg that had rolled there after Muntz's first fall. She grabbed it just as the VT pilot shook his head and leapt to his feet to face Bowie again.

His luck wasn't any better this time; Bowie was just out of the Academy, young and fast and in good shape. He rocked Muntz back with a left hook, and Muntz ended up knocking Marie Crystal back onto a couch, lying across her lap. While Marie pounded his head and howled at him to get off her, the riot got going in earnest.

As chairs were flung and punches thrown, kicks and leg-blocks vigorously exchanged, Dana suddenly realized what she had gotten herself and the 15th into.

And she stood numbly, watching a mental image of her lieutenant's bars as they flew away into the clouds forever on little wings. *I wonder if Sean's got any CARE packages to spare, there in the stockade?* she thought.

CHAPTER
FIVE

The occasion of the 15th's first social encounter with the Black Lions was rather less auspicious than subsequent, more cooperative military collaborations. It is a fact, though, that the ATACs ever thereafter insisted on referring among themselves to Veritech recons and penetration strikes in football-play jargon, as "Debutantes Go Long."

Zachary Fox, Jr., *Men, Women, Mecha: the Changed Landscape of the Second Robotech War*

DANA WAVED THE TABLE LEG, SHOUTING, "STOP! Stop this immediately!" It didn't do a bit of good.

The brawl was a confused sequence of split-second events; time and distance seemed strangely altered. A blond VT pilot swung his forearm into the face of a 15th trooper; another of Dana's men downed the mohawked Black Lion with a dropkick.

An ATAC was on the floor with a VT pilot's head in a leg lock; Shiro had Evans down and bent the wrong way, painfully, in a "Boston crab." Marie Crystal finally got the groggy Eddie Muntz off her just in time to have Louie Nichols and a VT man with whom he was locked in combat pile into her and bear her down in a struggling heap.

Dana couldn't think of anything to do but keep yelling "Stop! Stop!" and wave the table leg. It didn't accomplish much, and she had to stop even that and duck suddenly as a Black Lion flung bodily by Angelo Dante went crashing through the big window behind her.

The broken window let in a sound that made Dana's blood run cold: police sirens. An MP carrier was coming hell-for-leather across the field toward the canteen, all lights flashing. Dana turned and bellowed, "MPs! Hey, it's the MPs! Let's get outta here!"

Other voices took up the cry, and in seconds the brawl was over. Marie Crystal looked on as the 15th raced after its leader, hopping on Hovercycles. Dana made sure all her men had gotten out. "Split up! We'll meet back at the barracks!" The ATACs zoomed off in all directions.

Dana gunned her engine and headed off straight for the police van. It was closer now, an open surface-effect vehicle, and she could see that there was a fifteen-foot-tall police robot standing back on the troop carrier bed. Dana calmly watched the distance close; she was determined to keep the MPs busy until the rest of the 15th had time to get clear.

The MP major standing behind the open cab felt sudden misgivings as the cycle rider came straight at the van's windshield. He let out a squawk and went for his sidearm, steadying it at her with both hands over the top of the cab. "Stop or I'll shoot! *Look out!*"

The latter was because Dana had increased speed and hit her thrusters. The major dove for cover, thinking she was out to decapitate him. But at the last instant she took the cycle up in a thruster-jump, neatly tagging the police robot's head with the sky-scooter's tail. The robot toppled backward like a falling sequoia as the major screamed in horror. The sound the machine made against the hardtop resembled that of several boilers being rung like gongs.

The Black Lions stood outside the canteen, watching, as Dana threw them a jaunty wave and disappeared in the distance. Marie Crystal stood with hands on hips, a feline smile on her face. "Not bad for a beginner, Lieutenant Sterling. You show real promise." *And you haven't heard the last of the Black Lions!*

The MP van slowed to a stop. The major shook his head in disgust, watching the ATAC cycles leave dust trails to all points of the compass. *Doesn't the Academy teach these hoodlums the difference between us and the enemy?*

The robot lay unmoving, but its visor lit with red flashes with each word it spoke. "Hovercycle operator identified as Lieutenant Dana Sterling," the monotone voice announced, "Fifteenth ATAC squad." It made some strange noises, then added, "Recommend immediate apprehension. I don't feel very well. May we return to headquarters now? Perhaps you could give me a hand up, sir. *Vvvt! Wwarrrzzzp! Kktppsssst!* Reenlistment bonus? Sounds good to me!"

The major gave the robot a little first-echelon maintenance in the form of a good swift kick.

On a moonlit night with the silver veins of cloud overhead, Monument City had the look of a place transported to an eldritch graveyard. The wind-sculpted crags and peaks around it, the rusting dead leviathans of the Zentraedi wreckage, the barrenness of the countryside that began at the city limits—it all suited Dana's despair precisely.

Earlier that day she had led the 15th in a triumphant joyride up a curving concrete access ramp; now she crouched in an alley beneath it, in a part of the city where, she hoped, she could pass as just one more vagrant.

Sitting near the pile of refuse that concealed her cycle, hugging herself to conserve body heat, Dana sat with her back against a brick wall and tried to figure out what to do next. Eventually, she knew, she must return to the base and face the charges that would be brought against her; she just wanted some time to think things through. She was reassessing her entire concept of what it meant to be a commander.

Dana sighed and looked up at the cold, diamond-bright moon, and wondered whether Humans—whether she—would be fighting and dying there soon. If there was a war coming, as everybody was saying, she didn't have too much to fear from the MPs or a court-martial; the Southern Cross Army would need a capable young Hovertank officer too much to let her moulder in stir for very long. Besides, there was General Emerson, family friend and unofficial guardian, and though she hated the idea of asking for help, his influence could work wonders for her.

But she would be leading men and women into battle, and possible death; she *must not make any more misjudgments*. She hated being mocked and wronged, and she longed so very much to *connect* with something—perhaps her squadmates would be like the family she had never really known.

She sighed, pulling a holobead from an inner uniform pocket. Thumbing it in the dimness of the alley, she looked again on the image she had seen ten thousand times before.

There was Max Sterling, the greatest VT pilot who had ever lived, pale and boyish, with oversize corrective glasses and blue-dyed hair. Next to him was Miriya Parino Sterling, the woman who had commanded the Zentraedi's elite Quadrono Battalion, reduced from a giantess to Human proportions by a Protoculture sizing chamber, a woman with the predatory look of a tigress, and all the sleek beauty of one as well.

But they clung to each other lovingly, and between them they held a happy, blue-haired baby. Dana.

And now they're—who knows? she thought. She looked at the stars and reflected, as she did almost every night, that her mother and father might be beyond the most distant of them. Or might be dead. Few communications had been received from the SDF-3 expedition to find and deal with the Robotech Masters.

Dana pressed a minute switch, and the holobead showed its other image. An odd-looking trio stood there: Konda, tall and lean, with purple hair and an expression that said he knew something others didn't; Bron, big and broad, with such strong, callused hands and yet such a sweet, gentle nature; and Rico, small and wiry and fiery, dark-haired and mercurial.

Dana looked on them fondly; in front of them stood a Dana who was perhaps five, her hair its natural yellow color now, grinning and holding Bron's forefinger, squinting because the sun was in her eyes. The 15th's new—perhaps former, by now—CO heaved another sigh.

Konda and Bron and Rico were former Zentraedi spies, shrunk to Human size, who had fallen under the spell of Human society. Max and Miriya left with Rick Hunter, Captain Lisa Hayes, and the rest of the expedition in the SDF-3, and there was a certain lapse of time there that Dana couldn't account for and had been too young to remember—things that even General Emerson wasn't too forthcoming about. But eventually the erstwhile spies, learning that for some unexplained reason Max and Miriya had been persuaded to leave her behind, appointed themselves her godfathers.

A strange upbringing it was. No other person in history had been subjected to both Human and Zentraedi attitudes and teachings from infancy. The ex-spies were really only enlisted men, not well educated even for Zentraedi, whose whole history and lore were a Robotech Masters' concoction. Still, they taught her everything they could about her mother's people, and took better care of her than many natural parents could have done, in their own slightly bumbling, endearing way.

All the rebel Zentraedi—the ones who had defected to the Human side only to turn against the Earth again—had been hunted down while Dana was still an infant, and all the rest but her godfathers had gone along with SDF-3. Eventually the last three, her godfathers, passed away, almost at the same time. She was never certain whether it was from some Earthly malady or simply a vast loneliness; their three human loves, Sammie, Vanessa, and Kim, had died with Gloval and Bowie's aunt Claudia in the SDF-1's final battle. The ex-spies had never taken others.

With the trio gone, it was government youth shelters and schools for Dana once more, often with Bowie as her companion because Rolf Emerson simply couldn't have children along with him. And then, in time, there was the Academy. But when Dana heard bitter words about the innate savagery of the Zentraedi nature, she thought back on the one-time giants who had shown her such a happy family life, at least for a little while.

She deactivated the holobead with a stroke of her thumb, leaning her head back against the coarse bricks, eyes closed, taking in a deep breath through her nostrils. There were the distant lights of apartments, where families were getting together for dinner after a day of workaday life.

Dana let her breath out slowly, wishing again that she could be one of them, wishing that the holobead images could come to life, or that her parents would come home from the stars.

There was a sudden whimper and the hollow bounce of an empty can nearby. She was on her feet, reflexively ready for a fight. But there was no enemy there. It was, instead, a quite special acquaintance.

"Polly!"

She stopped to gather the little creature up, a thing that looked like a mophead, its tongue hanging out. It might have passed for a terrestrial dog until one took a closer look. It had small knob-ended horns, eyes that were hidden beneath its sheepdoglike forelock—but that were definitely not the eyes of an Earth lifeform—and feet resembling soft muffins.

It's a pollinator, Bron had told her gently the first time she was introduced to it. That's how she had given the thing its name, even though she had no idea whether Polly was male or female.

She never found out just how the ex-spies had come across the affectionate little beast; they had promised to tell her in the "someday" that had never come. But she had learned that Polly was a magical creature indeed.

For instance, Polly came and went as it pleased, no matter if you locked it in or tied it up. You would look around, and Polly would just be gone, maybe for a little while or maybe for a long time. It reminded her a little of *Alice's Adventures in Wonderland*, and later, another old-time book title she came across, *The Cat Who Walks Through Walls*.

The pollinator was her first adult-style secret, since her godfathers told her she must never mention it to anybody, and she had kept that secret all her life. Apparently, Polly was part of some miraculous thing, but she never found out what. Polly had managed to find her for brief visits four or five times since the death of Konda, Bron, and Rico.

"Did you hear me thinking about them?" she murmured, petting the XT creature, pressing her cheek to it as it licked her face with a red swatch of tongue. "Didja know how much I can use a slobber on the face just now?" Her tears leaked out no matter how she tried to hold them back. "Looks like we're both gonna be cold tonight."

She wiped her cheek, smearing the tears and dirt. "I can't believe I let things get so far out of control."

But somehow she felt less terrible. She managed to fall asleep, the pollinator curled up warmly against her. The dark dreams that came to her at times, filled with terrors that were both nameless and otherwise, stayed away this time.

But she had her strange Vision again, as she had had on rare occasions ever since she could remember. In it, a vortex of purest force swirled up from the planet Earth like the funnel of a cyclone; only it was a cyclone a hundred miles in diameter, composed of violent energies springing from sheer mental power. The uppermost part of the mind-tornado reached beyond Earth's atmosphere, then it suddenly transformed into an incandescent phoenix, a firebird of racial transfiguration.

The crackling, radiant phoenix spread wings wider than the planet, soaring away quicker than thought to another plane of existence, with a cry so magnificent and sad that Dana dreaded and yet was held in the powerful beauty of this recurring dream. Her Vision was another secret she had always kept to herself.

As Dana stirred in her sleep, something came between her and the streetlights. That struck through to a trained alertness that had long since become instinctive; she lay utterly still, opening one eye just a crack.

Looming over her was the person of Lieutenant Nova Satori of the Global Military Police. Backing her up were a half-dozen MP bruisers cradling riot guns. Some sort of dawn was trying to get through clouds that looked like they had been dumped out of a vacuum-cleaner bag. The pollinator was no longer lying against Dana.

Nova was enjoying herself. She was turned out in the MP dark-blue-and-mauve version of the Southern Cross dress uniform, her long blue-black hair fluttering and luffing against her thighs like a cloak, caught back with a tech ornament like Dana's.

In Nova's quick dark eyes and the heart-shaped face there was the canniness of both the cop and the professional soldier.

"Well, good morning," said Nova with a pleasant purr.

Funny how you run into old buddies when you least expect it, Dana reflected, and rose to her feet in one smooth move. She and Nova went back a long way. Dana put on her best Miss Southern Cross Army smile. "Well, Lieutenant Satori! How ya been? *You're* out early!"

Dana gave a completely false laugh while looking over possible escape routes as Nova said in a Cheshire cat voice, "Fine, just fine."

Polly was nowhere in sight, and there were no avenues of escape. *Uh-oh.*

In Southern Cross HQ, high up in one of the buildings that looked like crusaders' war-standards, the army's command center operated at a constant fever pitch, a twenty-four-hour-a-day steam bath of reports, sensor readouts, intelligence analysis, and system-wide surveillance.

Scores of techs sat at their consoles while diverse duty officers and NCOs passed among them, trying to keep everything coherent. Overhead, visual displays flashed on the inverted dome of the command center ceiling, showing mercator grid projections, models of activity in the Solar System, and current military hotspots.

On one trouble-board, ominous lights were blinking. An operations tech covered his headset mike with the palm of his hand and yelled, "Cap'n? Come take a look at this."

The ops captain bent down over the tech's shoulder and examined the screen. There was a complete garble of the usual computer-coded messages.

"It ain't comin' from the space station, sir," the tech

said. "It's like somebody's messing with satellite commo, but who? And from where, if you catch my drift, sir."

The captain frowned at the display and double-checked the alphanumerics. Then he spun and barked, "Get General Emerson over here ASAP!" The message was being relayed ASAP—as soon as possible—before he was done speaking.

The tech looked up at the ops captain. "What d'you guesstimate, sir? Y'figure it's those—"

"Let's hope not," the captain cut him off.

Space Station Liberty was like a colossal version of a child's rattle, hanging endlessly at Trojan Lagrange Point Five. It was humanity's sole link with the SDF-3 expeditionary force that had set out either to negotiate an end to hostilities or beat the Robotech Masters into submission.

Messages had been few and far between, but hope still thrived. Or at least it had until the Robotech Masters came.

A command center tech covered his mike and called to an operations officer, "Sir, I have a large unidentified paint."

But Major General Emerson, Chief of Staff, Ministry of Terrestrial Defense, was in the command center by then, and came to bend near the tech and the all-important screen. The ops officer, a captain, knew when it was politic to take a back seat to a flag-rank officer. Which was almost always.

Besides, this was Rolf Emerson, hero of a dozen pivotal battles in the Global Civil War, the Robotech War, and the Disorders that followed them. For all of that, he was soft-spoken and correct to the lowest-ranking subor-

dinate. The word was that he would have been supreme
commander—would have been a UEG senator for that
matter—long since, except that he hated political games.
In the final analysis he was a GI, albeit a brilliant one; the
men and women under his command respected him for it
and the politicians and supreme staff officers resented
him, determining that he would never get another star.

But he was far too valuable to waste, so he was in the
right place at the right time on a day when the Human
race needed him badly.

"Put it up on Central Display, please, Corporal," Rolf
Emerson requested quietly.

The object and its trajectory and the rest of the scanty
data appeared on the billboard-size central display
screen. There was a single soft whistle. "Big, bad UFO,"
Emerson heard a thirty-year vet NCO mutter.

"Fast, too," an intelligence major observed; she
grabbed up a handset and began punching in codes that
accessed her own chain of command.

"Sir, d'you think this has to do with the shootout out
by Moon Base?" the captain asked.

"Still too early to tell," Emerson grated. The captain
shut up.

The tech reported, reading his instruments. "According to computers, the UFO is a powered vehicle and it's
on an Earth-approach vector, estimated time of entry in
Earth atmosphere one hundred twenty-three minutes,
forty seconds...*mark*. Visual contact in approximately
three minutes."

"Give me a look at this thing," Emerson said in a low,
even voice that people around him had come to recognize
as one that brooked no failure. People jumped, babbled

computer languages, typed at touchpads, made order out of chaos. Not one of them would have changed places with Emerson. The atmosphere in the command center had officers and enlisted ratings loosening their tunic collars, coming to grips with the fact that the Main Event might just be coming up during their watch.

"We need to see what they look like," Emerson said to a senior signals NCO who was standing near. She was his imagery interpretation specialist, and she went to work at once, coordinating sensors and imagery-interpretation computers.

At a Southern Cross communications and sensor intel satellite, sensor dishes and detection spars swung and focused. Information was fed and rejiggered and processed, nearly a billion and a half (prewar) dollars worth of technology going full-choke to process data that ended up in front of a reedy young man who had been drafted only eight months before.

Colonel Green, one of Emerson's most trusted subordinates, barked, "Corporal Johnson, talk to me! Haven't you got anything yet?"

Johnson had gotten used to the brass screaming at him for answers; he had become imperturbable. He had gone from being a weird technofreak highschooler through a basic training that still gave him nightmares to a slot as one of the few people who *truly* understood how Liberty's equipment worked.

So Colonel Green didn't rattle Johnson; he had had to introduce any number of brass hats to the stark facts of reality. The instruments would show what they would show, or not, and there were only limited things Humans could do about it. The first thing you had to teach officers was yelling louder rarely helped.

"One moment, sir." The female imagery interpretation NCO came over to watch.

Johnson worked at his console furiously, more a magician than a technician, and was rewarded with a raw, distorted image. The officers looking over his shoulder would never appreciate how much finesse that had taken, but the senior sergeant did.

Then it was gone again. Johnson punched up the recording of the intercept and put it up on the huge main screen. "Sir, I had a visual but I lost it. Countermeasures maybe; I dunno. Playback on screen alpha.

Something was out there all right, something enormous and blockish and headed for Earth, something with more mass than anything Humans had ever put in the sky. Something whose power levels made all the indicators jump off the scales, and made all the watching Southern Cross higher-ups clench jaw muscles.

"Wish we could see that thing better," Colonel Green muttered. Whatever Johnson had picked up, it was artificial and fast-moving; the zaggies in the sensor image kept it from telling them much more.

And it's coming right our way, Emerson contemplated.

CHAPTER
SIX

*The importance and power of the Global Military Police—
the GMP—was directly attributable to the near-feudal nature
of Earthly society at that time. The GMP constituted the only
truly worldwide law-enforcement organization, and was a
check and balance on those who had at their disposal the tremendous power of Robotechnology. As a result, the GMP was
an organization with its own war machinery, combat forces,
and intelligence network.*

*A career in the GMP was a possible road to swift personal
advancement, but the recruit had to say farewell to all outside
friendships; such things could no longer exist for him or her.*

S. J. Fischer, *Legion of Light: a History of the Army of
the Southern Cross*

"WHAT COULD THAT THING *be*?" COLONEL
Green burst out. Emerson was already way ahead of him,
wondering what the hell might lie in the lee of the moon.

"Accelerating," Johnson said. A fine sweat had appeared on his brow. The display symbol for the intruder
was marking its progress with integrals coming much
more quickly. It was coming at Earth fast; it was nearly
upon Liberty.

Just then there was a tremendous surge through all the
sensor/commo apparatus, after which many indicators
went dead.

"Playing for keeps," Green observed.

An op near Johnson turned to yell, "Sir, we've lost

commo with Liberty: voice, visual, everything on the spectrum."

"Patch in whatever you have to, but *keep that bogie in sight*," Rolf said in measured tones. He turned to Lieutenant Colonel Rochelle, his adjutant. "Get everything you've got on red alert. Get all the ready-reactions set for possible XT warfare. Prime the Hovertanks especially, and the VTs. Gimme everything, right? *Everything!*"

Oh, Dana, Bowie! God keep you...

He swung to the intel major, whom he knew to be an internal security fink. "Use whatever code you have to, Jackie, and get me a UEG telequorum, right now." She looked away from his gaze at once, unable to meet it. Then she licked her lips, resettled her glasses, picked up a handset. She cradled the phone to her, turning her back to the others there in the command center, and punched out a code.

Green came up behind Emerson to whisper harshly, "If they're Zentraedi, d'you *really* think we stand any chance against them?"

"Don't sweat it, Colonel."

"But sir, we don't even know who they are or what they can do to—"

Rolf Emerson whirled on him angrily, then suddenly quieted. He rapped the knuckle of one forefinger against Green's ribbons, decorations from another war and another time. Emerson wore just about as many; they were two graying men listening to alarms, knowing it was the death knell of the everlasting peace they had fought and hoped for.

"This planet's *ours*, Ted."

"But, General, isn't there—"

"Earth is ours! Maybe they're Zentraedi; who cares? *This planet is ours!* Now go saddle up everything we've got groundside, and draw up a rapid deployment op-plan, 'cause we're gonna need one real bad."

Ten days went by, and Dana figured she had miscalculated her worth. Or else, possibly, was there to be no war? In any case, she mouldered in solitary confinement, against all expectation.

Hard rations of protein cracker and water scarcely affected her; things had been worse, *much* worse, on any number of training maneuvers; stockade was a cakewalk.

Mostly, she caught up on sleep, and worried about what was happening to the 15th, and stared out the window from her bunk. In her dreams there was a strange procession of images, and twice the haunting cry of the phoenix.

The door viewslit slid back; Dana recognized the eyes she saw there, and the limp blond hair around the face. Colonel Alan Fredericks said in a voice muffled by the door, "Accommodations to your liking, Ms. Sterling?"

Dana curled a lip at him. "Sure, it's home sweet home, sir."

Fredericks said, "I'm glad you've held up so well for ten days. Anything to say for yourself?"

Dana indicated her smudged face and rank, filthy uniform. "A hot bath and a change of clothes would feel nice. And maybe a manicure and a facial."

Fredericks allowed himself a thin smile. "No, no—we don't want you to be distracted from contemplation of your crimes, do we now?"

Dana sprang to her feet, holding her hands out to him imploringly. "Please let me return to my squad! Sir, we might be at war anytime now; I've got to be with the fifteenth!"

"Stop your whining!" Fredericks roared at her. "If it were up to me, you would have been drummed out of the Army of the Southern Cross!"

He sniggered. "Little Dana, daughter of the great heroes, Max and Miriya Sterling! It seems blood doesn't always tell, does it?"

Actually, Fredericks was of the opinion that breeding *did* tell, and was glad that this halfbreed had proved it. But he dared not say such a thing with guards nearby as witnesses.

Dana fell to her knees, nearly in tears, facing the cold eyes in the door viewslit. "Sir, I'm begging you: give me a chance to square things, to prove myself. I'll never disgrace my family name or break a reg again, I swear it—"

"Stop sniveling!" Fredericks shouted.

The truth was, there was pressure on him from higher up to release Dana. Some of it came from her regimental commander, who needed her, and some from the Judge Advocate General's office; the JAG thought ten days was more than enough. General Emerson had said a few words on her behalf in the right ears, too.

But there was yet another source of pressure, one that Fredericks hadn't quite been able to track down. Evidence pointed toward its coming through civilian channels—from very high up indeed in the scientific and research power structure. One name he heard had him surprised and cautious: Dr. Lazlo Zand.

Zand had been the disciple of Dr. Lang, the high priest

of Robotechnology. When Lang went off with Rick Hunter, Dana's parents, and the rest in the SDF-3, Zand remained behind. Now Zand's activities and whereabouts were so shrouded in mystery as to defy even Frederick's efforts at investigation.

"Since you're so repentant, perhaps I will see what I can do," Fredericks told Dana coldly. The viewslit slid shut.

Dana, back on her feet, thrust her fist high into the air. *"Yahooo!"*

It was less than an hour later when the door of her cell rolled open. Dana stepped into the corridor to find Colonel Fredericks giving her his best basilisk glare. He held a leather swagger stick that resembled a riding crop, of all things. Standing on the opposite side of the doorway was Nova Satori.

Someone else was approaching, being escorted by two rifle-toting guards. Fredericks had arranged the chance meeting to see what would happen.

"Hey, Dana!"

She whirled, and a sunny smile shone on her face. "Sean! What're you doing in solitary? No, don't tell me; you, ah, made a pass at a general's wife?"

Sean Phillips, erstwhile CO of the 15th, gave her one of his famous roguish grins. He was even more famous as a Don Juan than as a fighter, a tall, athletic twenty-three-year-old with a boyish haircut and long brown locks framing his face.

Sean gave her a wink. "Naw. They decided I needed a

little privacy, I guess; you know how it is when you're a celebrity. Besides, they're springing me tomorrow."

Nova caught a subtle signal from Fredericks, and barked, "Shut up and keep moving, Phillips!" The look on her face let everyone know that she was immune to his charms; she had put Sean in his place the moment he tried his Romeo routine on her. And the second time and the third.

Sean was shoved into the cell Dana had just vacated, and the door rolled shut. Nova told Dana, "Just screw up one more time, Lieutenant, and you won't even know what hit you."

Dana choked back the retort that came to her lips. "Yes, ma'am." She saluted the two MP officers, did a right face, and moved out.

"I don't trust either of them, Nova," Fredericks said quietly, slapping his palm with the swagger stick. "Keep me updated on her activities, and on Phillips's, too, once he's freed."

"Will do, sir."

Dana's release came just as the UEG made public the news of the aliens' appearance. It was a brief, tersely worded statement ending with the fact that the ship had taken up a geostationary orbit some twenty-three thousand miles out in space.

Of course, the entire Southern Cross Army was going to red alert; that was why she had been released. Dana soon found herself in a jeep with Nova Satori and two guards, being hustled back to the 15th. Her regimental commander wanted every Hovertank manned; there was some word that Sean might get an early release, too.

At a Southern Cross base, the silo blast doors were open and the Earth's most powerful missiles were primed. Captain Komodo, battalion commander, surveyed his instrumentation. He was a broad, powerful-looking man of Nisei descent, with a chestful of medals.

A fire-control tech looked up at him. "Sir, is there any word on who these aliens are?"

Komodo frowned. "It's obvious they're the same ones who attacked Moon Base. But now we're ready for them." Komodo had lost a brother in that raid; he hungered for revenge.

He spun to face a commo operator. "I told you to keep me informed! Well?"

The op shrugged helplessly. "No further orders, sir; we're still instructed to stand by."

"Fools!" muttered Komodo. "We have to strike *now*!" He reached down to flip up the red safety shields and expose a row of firing switches. Then Captain Komodo looked angrily into the sky, waiting.

At Southern Cross Command Headquarters, Emerson was in the eye of the storm.

"Sir, the alien's moving into a lower orbit," a tech reported.

"General, why are we waiting?" Green demanded. "With all due respect, sir, you must give the order to attack. Immediately!"

Emerson shook his head slowly, watching the displays. "It is imperative that we find out who they are and why they're here. We cannot fire first."

Green gritted his teeth. His hope that Supreme Commander Leonard or some other top brass would overrule Emerson had not come to pass. "But they killed our people, sir!"

Emerson turned to him. "I'm aware of that. But what proof do we have that Luna didn't bring the attack on itself by firing first? Do you want to start a war that nobody wants?"

Green swallowed his angry retort. He was old enough to remember the Zentraedis' first appearance and their disastrous onslaught.

So was Emerson; the general had seen enough war to dread starting one.

At the missile base the commo op looked to Captain Komodo. "Sir, the enemy spacecraft is descending from orbit—thirteen thousand miles and descending rapidly."

Komodo stood with teeth clenched, jaw muscles jumping. "Are you sure your equipment's working, Sparks? That there's been no command to open fire?"

"Affirmative, sir."

Komodo's fists shook. *If those cowards at headquarters would just work up the guts to give me the green light, I'd blow those aliens out of the sky!*

With the Earth an ocean-blue and cloud-white gem beneath it, the Robotech Masters' ship suddenly launched three sand-red objects shaped like pint whiskey bottles. Their thrusters howled, and they dove for the planet below.

"Captain, landing craft of some kind have left the mother ship and begun entry maneuvers."

Komodo looked over the fire-control tech's shoulder. "Got 'em on radar yet?"

"That's affirm, sir."

Komodo clapped a hand to the man's shoulder. "Good! I want A and B batteries to take out the mother ship first; it won't be launching any more sneak attacks. Charlie and Delta batts will target the attack craft."

The tech was looking at him wide-eyed. "What's wrong? I gave you a fire-mission!" Komodo shouted.

"But sir! HQ gave specific orders that—"

Komodo caught the hapless youngster up by his torso harness and flung him aside. "You idiot! You want to wait until they blow the whole planet away?" His fingers flew over the control console; in moments the ground trembled.

The huge, gleaming pylons—Skylord missiles—rose up in fountains of flame and smoke, shaking the base and the surrounding countryside.

The Robotech Masters proved themselves not to be infallible or invincible; though they vaporized two Skylords with charged particle beams, the other two got through, making brilliant flashes against the huge mother ship.

On Earth, Emerson and the others in the command center looked at their screens in astonishment. "Confirmed Southern Cross missile launch, sir," someone said. "Heavy damage thought to have been suffered by the enemy ship; sensors indicate they're floating dead in space."

Emerson turned on his subordinates with white-hot anger. "Who launched those birds?" There was confusion among them and, Emerson knew, no time to waste placing blame.

Now we're committed. "Open fire! Hit 'em with everything we can throw. Inform Supreme Commander Leonard and tell Civil Defense to get on the stick!"

"War," said Colonel Fredericks, savoring the word and
the idea. "Just my luck to be stuck here guarding a bunch
of underaged eightballs."

"Yes, sir," Nova answered. She wasn't quite as eager
to kill or be killed as her superior, but knew that it would
be wise to hide the fact.

"Still, little Dana should see some action," Fredericks
frowned, slapping his desktop with his swagger stick.
"Probably do her good, too."

He rose from his chair. "Well, let's see what we can do
to guarantee that, eh?"

The Skylords were all away; Captain Komodo stared
in fury as the screens showed him how, one after another,
they were blown to harmless mist by the energy weapons
of the descending enemy. Not surprisingly, the alien assault craft were homing in on the source of the missiles
that had damaged their mother ship.

"Fire!" Komodo bellowed, and rack after rack of
APC-mounted Swordfish missiles boiled away into the
air, leaving corkscrewing white trails. Tremendously powerful pulsed beams from the assault ships blasted them
out of the sky in twos and threes, while the aliens closed
in on the base.

Komodo gulped and watched the bottle-shaped vessels
come into visual range. He looked around him for a rifle
or a rocket launcher; he had no intention of running and
he had no intention of going down without a fight.

High above, access ports opened and enemy mecha swarmed out. Led by a red Bioroid like a crimson vision of death, the Masters' warriors dove their Hovercraft and sought targets, firing and firing.

CHAPTER
SEVEN

Hwup! Tup! Thrup! Fo'!
Alpha! Tact'l! Armored! Corps!
For-git Jody! For-git Dotty!
Ay-tacks OWNS yo' student body!

> Cadence chant popular among ATAC drill instructors

IN THE READY-ROOM OF THE 15TH SQUAD, ATAC, Trooper Winston was sitting with chin on palm and gazing at his squadmates sourly. "Finally, the balloon goes up—and we're stuck here!"

Next to him, Coslow, arms folded on his chest, nodded. "Why's it always our turn in the barrel?"

Angelo Dante nodded. "All this terrific talent being wasted just 'cause both of our officers happen to be doing bad time."

They weren't even suited up in armor. Express orders from Higher Up said that no Hovertank outfit would be allowed into a combat situation without a commissioned officer—preferably an Academy-trained one—in command.

Bowie, pacing, crossed to Angelo. "Why don't they just let *you* take over, Sergeant?"

Angelo sighed philosophically and shook his head. "I'd love it, kid, but there's just no way, know what I mean?"

Any Hovertanker knew the drills and could act independently on a combat mission—could even take over command if it came to that—but the Hovertanks had to be able to do more. The knowhow to integrate with other types of mecha, with TASC units like the Black Lions and so forth; to interpret complex tactical scenarios; to understand the various commo computer languages; to see, in short, the Hovertank's mission in terms of an entire Southern Cross op-plan, and to work to the maximum benefit of that overall plan was something that took years of study—study Angelo hadn't received.

Angelo raised his shoulders, dropped them. "This isn't one of Dana's drills. There's gonna be lives on the line this time, Bowie."

Not to mention one of the first fully operational Hovertank outfits in the Southern Cross, a huge investment of time and treasure and technology. The UEG's newest combat arm *must* serve well and protect the people who had paid its price tag.

Louie Nichols was polishing his sidearm again. Word had it that he had figured out an unauthorized modification that would triple the power of its pulses; people edged away from him when he played with the handgun, not wanting to be at ground zero in case Louie overlooked some potential glitch.

"No offense, Angelo," Louie said, "but I'm a little too busy to die right now."

"Anyhow, thanks for the vote of confidence, Bowie," Angelo finished.

Just then the door to the ready-room parted and there

stood Dana, in full spit-shined combat armor lacquered white, black, and scarlet, her helmet in the crook of her left arm. The armor, all ultratech alloy, somehow had the look of an earlier day to it—a flaring at the hips and shoulders that suggested both jousting panoply and whalebone corsetry.

"Fall in!"

The 15th's collective mouth hung open. Angelo came to his feet. "I thought you were doing thirty days bad time. You're not serious, right?"

Dana beamed. "Wrong again. Crank it up, Fifteenth! We're heading for a hotspot, to stop the enemy or die trying!"

Angelo released a deep breath. "Yes ma'am." *But dying under the command of a diz-zo-max teenager—it isn't exactly the way I'd hoped to go out.*

Louie walked by, holstering the pistol, eyes hidden in the dark goggles. "Well, when the whistle blows, everybody goes, Angie, so let's get goin'!"

This time they took the drop-rack one level deeper, leaping clear amid the Hovertank parking bays as the lights came up to full brightness. All were armored now, dashing to their craft with the sureness of constant drill. The overhead lights flashed white, red, white, red, to indicate the 15th was rolling on a priority wartime deployment.

The Hovertanks were bigger than their pre-Robotech counterparts, and heavier; yet they lifted lightly on thrusters, turning end-for-end like pirouetting rhinos, very maneuverable and responsive. The 15th handled their mecha with manual controls; there was no need for the thinking caps yet.

The bulky war machines followed as Dana led the way in her command tank, the *Valkyrie*, shooting up the access tunnel, following the glowing traffic-routing arrows embedded in the pavement.

They left the base and the city behind, heading for their assigned objective. The Hovertanks took up a precise skirmishing formation behind her. The mecha's headlights, under the downward sweep of the forward cowling, gave them the look of angry crabs.

Today I show them I've got what it takes. Dana steeled herself.

"Fifteenth squad will proceed ASAP to sector Q, I say again, Q for Quebec." The order came over the command net. "Suspected alien landing site. Use extreme caution."

"'Kay; you all know what to do," Dana told her ATACs. But inwardly she winced. *Alien!* I'm *half alien, and I'm on my way out to put my hide on the line for this planet, you sorry sack!*

Yeah, now this is where I belong, Angelo thought, the wind harsh in his face, the tank shrilling beneath him.

The Hovertanks were assemblages of heavy-gauge armor in angular, flattened shapes and acute edges, with rounded, downsloping prows, riding thruster pods. The angles, as in armor throughout history, were for deflection of rounds aimed at the tanks.

The Hovertanks kicked up huge plumes of dust as they raced to sector Quebec. Long before they got there, the members of the 15th could see that they had drawn a hotspot; explosions blossomed as detonations threw debris high in the distance, while energy beams drew angry lines through the air.

They topped a rise and looked down on a smoking

battlefield. Scattered all around were blasted and burning scraps of war mecha, almost all of Earthly origin. A Civil Defense Flying Corps outfit was manning outmoded ten-year-old VTs. The aircraft had come to life and assumed Battloid configuration, but they lacked the size, firepower, and groundfighting ability to deal with the ravaging XT mecha.

A tiny part of the enemy's telemetry had been intercepted, most of it impenetrable. But using certain old Zentraedi decryption programs, the code breakers had come up with what they thought was the designation of the invaders' war machines: Bioroids.

Dana pulled on her helmet/thinking cap, which featured graceful wings at either side, and a curved crest like a steel rainbow along its center. As she made it fast to her armor, it sealed and became airtight; so protected, she could survive radiation, chemical agents, water, vacuum, high pressure—almost any hostile environment. The wings and crest gave her a look that validated the name with which she had christened her tank, *Valkyrie*.

"Here we go!"

She gunned her tank's power plant, then set off, leading the way. The 15th raced after her.

Down below, the CDs were doing badly. The enemy mecha were drubbing them terribly; as the 15th watched, two blue giants led by a red one, all riding the flying-saucer Hoverplatforms like futuristic charioteers or alien water-skiers, stooped for another kill.

As the tankers charged in, the Bioroid trio led by the red one swooped in at two VTs who stood their ground in Battloid configuration. The red Bioroid, in the lead, fired quick, accurate bursts with the gun mounted on its control stem, and blew two of the VTs away, easily avoiding most of their fire and shrugging off the rest.

The Hovertanks were in the air now. "Switch to Gladiator mode!" Dana called over the tac net. In midair the tanks shifted, reconfigured, *mechamorphosed*. When they landed, they were squat, two-legged, waddling gun turrets the size of a house, each with a single massive cannon stretching out before it. The big guns were the mecha's primary batteries, even more powerful than the tank cannon.

The Gladiators fired, shoulder to shoulder. It was like a cannonade from the heaviest artillery. Two blue Bioroids went up in furious explosions, then a third. Another jumped clear of its Hoverplatform just as the platform was blown to bits. The Bioroid fired in midair, with a Bioroid-size pistol shaped something like a fat discus held edge-on, and took cover immediately when it hit the ground.

Other Bioroids were already there, having seen what intense fire the Gladiators could throw into the air. The aliens set up a determined counter-fire with Bioroid small-arms.

Dana took a deep breath and hopped her Gladiator high, imaging the move through her thinking cap. She landed to one end of a Bioroid firing line to set up an enfilade. But an alien had spotted her, and swung to fire. Dana got off the first shot and holed the outworld mecha through and through with a brilliant lance of energy that left glowing, molten metal around the edges of the point of entry.

"Gotcha!"

The Bioroids continued a stubborn, grudging resistance, but it was clear at once that the Hovertank Gladiators had advantages the Veritech Battloids didn't. They were bigger, more powerful, and more heavily armored, and carried greater firepower. On the ground, slugging it out toe to toe, the Bioroids had met their match.

Deafening volleys of nova cannonfire hammered back and forth in the little valley; Bioroids fell, discovering that without their Hovercraft they were on an equal footing with the ATACs.

The firefight raged on, neither side gaining or losing much ground. Suddenly, the red Bioroid leapt high from its position behind the blues. Showing great dexterity, it avoided the few cannon rounds that the startled Gladiators got off at it, to land between two 15th mecha. It blasted one at point-blank range, and turned to fire at the second even as the other Gladiator swung its barrel around desperately.

The red Bioroid fired into the second Gladiator while the first was erupting in a fireball; the second Earth mecha, too, went up in a groundshaking explosion. The red jumped again, to continue its awesome offensive.

Dana shook herself to get over the shock of it; two troopers dead in seconds, two mecha utterly destroyed, and the red bounding on to attack again. *All right, Dana!* she told herself firmly. *Show 'em what you've got!* "Dante, switch your team to Battloid mode, *now!*"

She did the same, jumping her mecha to a better firing position. The craft went through mechamorphosis in midair, taking on the form of a huge Human-shaped battleship, an ultratech knight. Half the 15th reared up now in Battloid form, the remainder hunkered down in Gladiator to give fire support.

The blue Bioroids seemed daunted, surprised at the mechamorphosis and unsure about coming to grips with the Humaniform machines. But the red Bioroid carried the attack once more, aiming the massive disc-pistol at Dana and unleashing a raging bolt of energy.

"Oh, no, y'don't!" She jumped her Battloid high as the shot annihilated the ground where she had stood. At her command the Battloid took its plasma rifle—which was the tank's cannon now reconfigured—into its hands as it flew through the air. Dana fired on the fly, muttering, "Now it's *your* turn!"

The red ducked, then raced to meet her as her Battloid landed with a deft flip. In moments they were ducking it out in the rocks nearby, springing up to fire at each other, then diving for cover again, while the rest of the 15th engaged the invaders once more. Without the red to lead them, the blues' assault faltered.

But in the meantime, Dana was fighting a desperate duel against a very capable foe. What's more, she couldn't lose the strange feeling that she *knew* this machine, knew something all-important and fateful about it. It was stronger than mere déjà vu, more like an emphatic Vision.

She spotted Louie Nichols's Gladiator on the cliffs above her. "Gimme some covering fire, Louie!"

"Yo!" The magnification in Louie's goggles was at normal, and they were letting in all available light even though they were still opaque from the outside. He relied on his tank's range finder rather than on the one in his goggles as he swung hard on the steering grips, imaged the shot through his helmet receptors, and got ready to let one off.

The red spied him just as he took aim, and leapt. Louie was so busy trying for the shot, trying to lead his bounding target just right, he didn't realize one of the assault craft had swung in low over the battle.

The cannon round hit the craft's underbelly almost dead center, jolting it—perhaps the most bizarre event of a bizarre day. The Bioroids halted, seemed to listen to something, and began retreating.

In moments their Hovercraft came to the surviving invaders, summoning them like faithful hunting hounds. The enemy mecha jumped aboard, and raced for their ship. As it turned to go, the red Bioroid paused to look at Dana one last time. It seemed to be staring right into her eyes, thinking thoughts that were meant for her. Once more she had the strange sensation, like some impossible memory, that she and the foe had some essential bond.

"We did it, Lieutenant!" Angelo called out, elated, over the tac net. "Not bad for a baptism of fire!"

"Sir, all enemy mecha and landing craft have withdrawn," Green reported to Rolf Emerson. "They ran for it as if they weren't going to stop until they were home. The mother ship has moved back to a geostationary orbit. You were right, General; we sent them packing once before and today we did it again! All units are at yellow alert and awaiting further orders."

Emerson turned from his contemplation of Monument City. "G2 Intelligence staff has concluded, and I concur, that the aliens are here for our Protoculture supply, gentlemen. You may be sure that we will see them again."

Lieutenant Colonel Rochelle, Emerson's adjutant,

looked dismayed. Colonel Green said gruffly, "Let 'em!
My boys and girls're ready, anytime!"

But it was depressing news. Protoculture was essential
to the operation of Robotechnology, and the Earth's supply was limited. As far as Humans knew, all that remained of it was what was left after the Robotech War.
The Zentraedi had originally invaded Earth to claim the
Protoculture Matrix from Zor's crashed ship, but subsequent investigation had failed to turn up anything. It
seemed the last remaining means for the actual production of Protoculture was gone forever.

Zentraedi and Humans alike were unaware of what lay
beneath the three burial mounds near the ruins of Macross City—of the trio of wraiths who guarded the
wreckage of the SDFs 1 and 2 and Khyron's vessel, and
the unique treasure they protected.

"Damage report?" Emerson said.

"Fighting was contained to unpopulated areas," Green
answered."

"Minimal losses; Fifteen ATAC squad stopped those
aliens' butts *cold*, sir," Rochelle added.

Emerson nodded. "The Fifteenth, hmm? Looks like
Lieutenant Phillips gets himself another commendation."

Rochelle *ahemm*ed. "He wasn't there, sir; they didn't
get him out of the slammer in time. Lieutenant Dana
Sterling led the squad today."

Emerson permitted himself a proud smile. "Ah, Dana.
Yes."

The drudgery of checking over all their mecha and
equipment after the battle, preparing to go into combat
again at a moment's notice, was sobering work to the

15th. They had won, but they had taken losses, too: dead and wounded who might easily have been any of those who came through unscathed.

After they got the order to stand down, they worked, fighting every instant and every portion of the battle again, over and over, among themselves; recounting and arguing, joking and lamenting.

It was still going on up in the ready-room, when the door opened and Sean Phillips walked in, escorted by Nova Satori. "Hi, guys. Life pretty boring without me around, was it?"

"We managed to keep ourselves occupied." Louie grinned.

Nova snapped, "By order of the commander, Alpha Tactical Armored Corps, Sean Phillips is reduced to the rank of private, second class."

Everyone in the room gasped. Nova went on. "And as for you, Sterling—"

Dana snapped to attention. "Whatever I did this time, ma'am, I'm ready and willing to accept disciplinary action."

"Quiet!" Nova barked. "You've been promoted to permanent command of the Fifteenth, Lieutenant. Don't blow this chance, because I'll be keeping an eye on you." Nova turned and exited. Except for Sean, everybody there was watching Dana.

The computer-controlled bar that dispensed only non-alcoholic drinks to those on duty was ready to serve something a little stronger. Sean had already eased over to it, and was taking a long pull from a tall glass. "Private Second Class Phillips!"

Sean spat out part of his drink as Dana shouted his name. "*I'll* be watching *you*," she told him.

Sean looked startled, then gave her a dose of the famous grin. "Just give the word. I'm yours to command, Lieutenant."

There was knowing laughter and some catcalling from the rest of the 15th, but Dana was satisfied that the point was made, and that everyone accepted the change of command. She couldn't afford to have Sean second-guessing her, or having her troops expect him to.

Sean was a great soldier and a definite asset, but she didn't think much of the idea of putting a busted CO back in the outfit he had commanded. But it looked like she would have to live with it.

Later, in the shower, she ran over the things she would have to get done as soon as possible. Replacements for the casualties and the destroyed Hovertanks would be coming in, and she would have to do some reshuffling of her Table of Organization and Equipment. There would be training and more training, to make the 15th a well-integrated fighting unit once more—and little time to do it in.

In the midst of all her ruminations she suddenly stopped, standing stiffly, immobilized. As vividly as if it were actually there before her, she saw the red Bioroid again . . . felt again that strange sensation of a bond between them.

CHAPTER
EIGHT

> *I am satisfied that I've now ended any blasphemous talk of treating with the aliens, either among my subordinates or the Council. These aliens are an abomination, a violation of the Divine Plan; we must exterminate them all. That is our holy obligation.*

> From the personal journal of Supreme Commander Anatole Leonard

REASSURING MEDIA ANNOUNCEMENTS OF THE SITUation were quickly followed by a formal declaration of war. The armored troops posted on street corners and patrolling everywhere were more for the civilians' peace of mind than any deterrent value.

But the Human race had been very much a military culture since the Global Civil War and, organized along feudal lines under the UEG, accepted the necessity that it must fight once again.

"Headquarters' thinking is that we can't sit around and wait for them to make the next move," Rochelle told the assembled officers. "The opinion is that their Robotechnology and scientific edge outweighs our numbers and home-field advantage. We've got to start calling the play —draw them out with fighters, lay in a missile barrage on that flagship. We've got to keep them off balance."

"It's just not in our blood to sit and wait for them to call all the shots," a G3 light-colonel agreed.

A G2 intel major took off his glasses, shaking his head. "But their counterattack might end up annihilating our entire defense force, don't you understand that?"

"That's right, it's insane to attack now! It's like jabbing a stick into a hornets' nest—a very *short* stick," a recon captain laughed harshly.

"That will do!" Rochelle bit out the words, and the assembled officers subsided. Dana looked up and down the table, studying them.

Marie Crystal was there; so was Fredericks. So were some other ATACs people, some Civil Defense—it was odd to know that her unit's survival might depend on these people, or theirs on her.

"The decision has been made," Rochelle went on. "You in this Strikeforce will carry the war to the enemy. Lieutenant Sterling's squad will handle rear guard and provide an entrenched fall-back position. There will be additional coverage from nearby missile and artillery bases and the various ready-reaction units. Lieutenant Crystal, your Black Lions will be our spearhead."

They already knew the plan, had the briefing files before them and the tactical displays on screens around the room, but he reviewed for them one more time anyway. When he was finished, Marie said, "We'll be ready, sir."

Dana made a sour face. "Some people have all the luck. Don't get your tail shot off, Marie." Marie slipped her a wink.

"Colonel Fredericks," Rochelle was saying, "I'm putting these units and their installations on red alert as of now; I want the bases sealed and a full commo blackout imposed. This attack has to come as a complete surprise. No one enters or leaves or communicates with outsiders in any way except by my direct order, understood?"

Fredericks seemed to be savoring the idea of having his MPs coop up the Strikeforce troops and make them toe the line. "Most affirmative, sir; you can count on it."

Sean Phillips snarled, "Somebody tell me what's goin' on here!"

He stood with fists cocked by the Hovertank parking bays, glowering at Louie Nichols and a few of the others who were running maintenance.

"I d-didn't want to bring it up," Louie fumbled, familiar with Sean's tripwire temper. "That is, uh—"

"As of today, you've been assigned to a new Hovertank," Bowie intervened.

"Somebody slipped up," Louie hastened. "With you bein' in the brig and all. Guess they forgot to tell you." Sean grabbed a handful of Louie's uniform and pushed him back against a tank, growling like an angry wolverine.

Sean's tank, the *Queen Maeve*, was his pride and joy, finely tuned so that it ran like a watch, lovingly maintained in every way. That made it that much more undesirable, in Louie's estimation, to be the one to tell him what had happened.

Louie yelped, and Bowie hollered, "Cut it out, Phillips!" But before anyone could break it up, Sean dropped the lanky tech-freak and wheeled, eyes roving the bays.

"Listen, they sent in a new guy from the replacement depot when you went in the stockade," Louie confessed, rubbing his chest. "Then Dana got put in command and then they jailed her and then they sprang her and made her CO—in all the confusion, the repple-depple new guy got *Queen Maeve*. And *he* was one of the guys who didn't make it, Sean."

"Your tank's in about a thousand pieces, what's left of it," Bowie added.

"So which one's mine now?" Sean seethed. Then his eyes fell on a shrouded object in an end bay. "Ah! What's that? That mine?" He ran to it before anybody could tell him the truth.

Sean dragged the cover off, losing balance and falling on his rear. He sat, looking up in amazement. It was a new tank right off the production line, a gleaming war mecha with all the latest in Robotechnology refinements.

"Oh-hh," he breathed reverently. In another moment he was clambering aboard, laughing with delight. Bowie and Louie came dashing over.

"Beautiful, isn't it?" Louie said. He and Bowie traded resigned looks; there was going to be trouble.

"Man, this baby was built with me in mind!" Sean chuckled, running his hands over the controls, checking out the cockpit. "What a sweetheart! Nobody else in the Fifteenth could handle this darlin'—"

"But I'm afraid somebody else is going to have to try, *Private* Phillips," a voice said icily. Dana stood nearby, arms akimbo.

Sean leaned back in the pilot's seat, interlocking his fingers, staring off at the ceiling and ignoring her. "Nope."

Dana came over to stand beside the *Valkyrie*'s high-sheen side. "This tank's reserved for officer use, get it?

Read my lips while I repeat this, Private: you'll never fly this craft."

So the honeymoon was over and it was time to really decide who ran things in the 15th. And Dana held every ace. Recalling how much Fredericks seemed to enjoy having him as a houseguest down at Barbed Wire City, Sean resigned himself. "Damn it all, there ain't no justice in this world."

Bowie and Louie and some of the others were just barely stifling their laughter. "This tin can and me woulda been history on wheels. But—" He looked to Dana. "'Course, there's still a chance for you and me, little darlin'."

She had been waiting for that. Sean had been decent enough to her as a CO, had never put any moves on her —but that was before he wanted something from her. "The only history we'll make is when I send your sorry tail back to the stockade for insubordination, hotshot."

He knew her well enough to realize she would do it. Some females just didn't know how to be friendly. Sean hopped out of the tank. "All right; lay off. I was only thinkin' of the good o' the Corps. So, what'm I supposed to use as a ride?"

She gave him an innocent expression and pointed. "Look right up there."

Sean let out a curse. "That crate? The *Bad News*? That's the oldest junker we've got!"

"And it's all yours, Private; you'd better get to work on it."

Sean heaved a deep sigh. "Thanks."

"Now, listen up, everybody," Dana went on. "Orders from High Command. We move out at thirteen hundred hours tomorrow. The brass decided it's time we whip some hurt on these invaders."

There were the usual snafus, the usual hurry-up-and-waits, but all units were in place only slightly after the scheduled zero hour.

For some reason, the Strikeforce commander changed his mind at the last moment, ordering another TASC unit to go in as first attack wave. Marie Crystal stood in the base control tower and watched the VTs of the Redhawk Team take off.

In the 15th's ready-room, the tankers waited in full armor, helmets in hand. Dana strained to catch a glimpse of the fighters rising from the distant Fokker Base. *Man, I hate this waiting in the background! This is driving me zooey.*

"What's the matter, Lieutenant?" Louie Nichols smirked. "Pulling reserve duty doesn't agree with you?"

"Sometimes it's tough to just stand pat," Angelo hinted.

Dana whirled on them. "As you were! I don't need to be reminded what my orders are!"

At that moment the PA squawked, and they got the order to move out. The 15th was among the very last units to be moved into place as Southern Cross command made some final arrangements in defensive deployment.

The tankers charged for the drop-rack, and in moments they were tearing down the highway, bound for an industrial area at the edge of Monument City. The 15th went with helmets off for the time being; manual controls would suffice for a mere drive from point A to point B.

Playing shuttlecars, is that *all we're going to get to do?*
Dana fumed.

The Redhawk VTs came up in a ballistic climb, then
formed up for attack and headed straight for the alien. In
the command center, Emerson and his staff studied a visual image of the underside of the Robotech Masters'
flagship.

It was an elongated hexagon, a huge lozenge of alloy
the size of a city, its superstructural features as big as
sportsdomes and skyscrapers. The blinking of its white
and purple running lights—if that was what the lights
were—was the only sign of activity in the ship.

"No doubt their sensors have detected the Redhawks,
sir," Colonel Green said.

"Attack begins in thirty seconds," Rochelle reported.
"I wonder what they'll throw back at us?"

Emerson leaned forward to call down to an officer on
the operations floor below. "Are you sure you haven't
picked up any reaction from the alien?"

The officer surveyed the consoles manned by his techs,
and the main displays big as movie screens. "That's affirmative, sir; no response of any kind."

Few things could have troubled Rolf Emerson more,
but it was too late. The screens began relaying visual
transmissions from VT gunpod cameras as the fighters
went in. One flight broke off to make a pass over the
enemy's upper hull, to size up the objective and draw fire
so that a second flight could make suppression runs on
the alien batteries.

The cameras showed conical structures the size of pyr-
amids, poking up out of a landscape of systemry. There

were ziggurats, onion domes, and towers like two-tined forks. But the ship remained silent and unresponsive, inert except for the lights. Two more passes didn't change that.

Emerson knew things had gone too far to simply pull back now. If he didn't give the order, Leonard or someone else farther up the line would. "All right; we'll *provoke* a response. Commence attack immediately."

The VTs swept in, releasing dozens of Mongoose missiles. The missiles were powerful and accurate, producing brilliant explosions and lots of smoke, but when the smoke cleared, it was evident that they had caused no detectable damage, none at all.

Then someone said, "Sir, I'm getting some movement from the enemy ship."

"Right." The Redhawks' leader could see them, too, now: elongated, bulbous things like inverted teardrops, looking more glassy than metallic, gracefully grooved with spiral flutings. They reminded some Human observers of chandelier light bulbs, emerging from housings or rising up from where they had lain flat along the hull, to come to bear on the fighters.

"Everybody look sharp for antiaircraft fire," the Redhawk leader said, though he had the feeling that those were more than just some AA guns snouting out to track his squadron.

The green-white serpentine discharges of energy bolts crackled from the long muzzles, writhing and intertwining like living things. All at once they were coming from everywhere, the invader ship protected by a blazing network of interlacing streams of destruction. One VT was blown to bits, then another, and two more, before the pilots could get clear.

Someone said, "Sir, I'm picking up an unidentified craft emerging from the mother ship; ID signature indicates one of their assault craft. Correction: make that *two* assault ships."

The XT craft zoomed out together and pounced on the VTs even as the Redhawk leader was warning his men. A pair of VTs attempting to strafe a cannon emplacement was taken from behind, blown to flaming wreckage by streams of green-white energy discs.

Emerson ordered the Redhawk leader, "Break off the attack on the mother ship and get on those assault craft at once! Keep them from getting back to the mother ship or reaching any ground targets."

"I copy, sir." But the VT leader didn't sound very confident about it.

Green told Emerson, "Sensor data indicate the power in each of those landing craft is superior to that in the entire Redhawk squadron."

"I'm not surprised, Colonel," Emerson said. "But it's not just a question of raw power. If we can isolate them —who knows?" Sufficient firepower concentrated in the right place might do the trick; one torpedo could sink a carrier, after all; one rocket could destroy an arsenal.

The Redhawks caught up with one of the assault craft on its plummet to the ground; they were having a hard time spotting the second.

"Okay, we've got 'im now; keep 'im in sight," the leader said, moving into position for a shot at the invader's tail. The VTs' guns hosed green-white energy discs much like the aliens'; it was Robotechnology against Robotechnology.

But the target was gone abruptly. The Redhawk leader craned to see what had happened. "Where'd he go?"

He got his answer a moment later. The landing boat had gone into an incredibly powerful dive, looped, and come around onto the Redhawk formation's tail.

"Break and shake!" yelled the leader, but it was too late to evade. The alien picked off the rear ship in the diamond of four, and went in after the others. A second burst from the invader got another VT and sent it plowing into its wingmate.

The leader came in for a high deflection shot at the bandit, but it evaded with amazing agility and slid around onto his tail, chopping away at him. The tight packages of destructive energy holed the fighter's fuselage, and sent the Redhawk leader plunging to the Earth, trailing flame and smoke.

The fighting had brought the ships down close to the ground; there was no time to eject.

Sean Phillips watched the Redhawk leader's VT plow into the ground, off in the distance, toward the air base.

"My God! Unbelievable! A whole squadron wiped out in two-three minutes!"

Angelo Dante shook his head slowly. "Maybe we didn't beat them the other day after all; maybe they just wanted to wait for the Main Event."

"We did beat them once, and we can beat them again," Dana contradicted loudly. But a moment later she gasped as she saw the second assault ship link up with the first. They turned and began an approach on the base, the origin of the fighters that had attacked their flagship. As they went they began dropping Bioroids, the mecha dispersing and advancing on their antigrav Hovercraft for an attack.

And at the head of the mountainous, armored invaders rode the red Bioroid.

CHAPTER
NINE

A WW I biplane had perhaps fifteen gauges and instruments, a WW II fighter some thirty-five or so. By the time of the Global Civil War, a front-line fighter-bomber had approximately four hundred indicators, readouts, and so forth. Robotech mecha made those planes look as simple as unicycles. Is it any wonder that the RDF, and the Southern Cross Army that took its place, had little use for people with fast reflexes and the rest of it, but who couldn't image, *couldn't* think *their mecha through a fight? It was the only conceivable way of controlling such an instrumentality.*

And even that wasn't always enough.

Zachary Fox, Jr., *Men, Women, Mecha: the Changed Landscape of the Second Robotech War*

THE CONVENTIONAL ARMORED VEHICLES AND SELF-propelled artillery at the base did their best to send up defensive barrages, but the Bioroids were too agile and their counterfire too devastating. The Bioroids wove down through the tracers and solid-projectile fire, and then opened up.

Blasts from the discus-shaped hand weapons sent the field pieces and battle tanks up in violent ruin. The missile batteries didn't have any better luck; more Bioroids came in at low angles, taking them out with highly accurate fire.

Pilots scrambled to their planes, horrified that they had been caught on the ground by the incredible speed of the alien attack. Men and women with one foot in the cockpit, or just lowering the canopy, or beginning their taxi, were incinerated in their exploding aircraft. Whole lines of parked ships disappeared in tremendous outlashings of energy. Armored leg infantry, bravely attempting to defend the base with small arms, were mowed down on strafing runs.

The Bioroids began cutting the base to ribbons, determined to turn it into one huge funeral pyre, beaming down communications and sensor towers, strafing barracks, savaging every target they saw.

One of the few TASC units to make it upstairs was Marie Crystal's. She formed up the Black Lions, then brought them around to do whatever they could in the face of the appalling counterattack.

They spied a flight of blue Bioroids led by the red. "Okay, nail those bastards!" she yelled; the VTs went in. But the Bioroids on their flying platforms were fearless and capable; they came head-on, knocking down first one Lion, then another.

But the VTs got on the scoreboard, too; Marie waxed a blue thoroughly, saw it fall in burning pieces along with its broken sky-sled. Another blue fell like a blazing comet, and the dogfight intensified. But Marie had a moment to notice that the red leader had disappeared, had gone on, she supposed, to direct the attack on the base.

But she couldn't break loose to give chase; just then two more blues jumped her.

Far across the valley, on the outskirts of Monument City, the 15th watched smoke rise from the airfield. It was obvious to them all now that the attack was completely concentrated there, but they received no orders to move in the midst of the turmoil. Dana could only guess what a madhouse the command center must be at the moment. Apparently nobody had stopped to think that the Hover-tanks were needed. That, or the message had never gotten through.

"Those dirty, murderous—" Bowie grated.

Dana made a decision. "Let's mount up."

That left Sean and Angelo to stare at her in amazement while she scrambled aboard her gleaming *Valkyrie*. Other 15th troopers raced to get rolling.

As *Valkyrie* eased forward on its surface-effect thrusters, Angelo moved to block the way. "No! Have you gone crazy?"

Dana throttled back, the tank settling, the pitch of its engines dropping. "Outta my way, Sergeant."

"We're assigned to protect this sector, Lieutenant. Or have you forgotten those orders?"

She stared down at him from her cockpit-turret. "What, so they can rip us apart one unit at a time? The commo nets are useless, and there *is* such a thing as personal initiative."

Angelo lowered his head like a bull to glare at her. "Our orders are to wait right here."

She gunned the tank again. "Then *you* can wait here, and remind 'em of that at my court-martial, Angie."

The big sergeant had to dive aside as the 15th followed Dana, screaming off to the battle. Sean, arms folded, was watching him. "You know she's gonna end up right back in the brig," Angelo said bitterly.

"Assuming we still *have* a brig." Sean smiled. Then he was boarding the *Bad News*. "See ya later, Sergeant."

Angelo was left to scratch his head, dumbfounded, as Sean hurried to catch up with the others. Then he heard another voice, a very strident one.

"Lieutenant, you are deserting your post! Return at once! Acknowledge!"

Nova Satori was pulling up on an MP Hovercycle, her blue-black hair billowing behind her under the confinement of her goggle band. She was yelling into a radio mike. With the communications systems so completely bollixed up—both from confusion and damage done by the raiders—she had been pressed into service as a messenger.

"Get back here or face a general court-martial!" she called, but she stopped the cycle near Angie's tank; it was pointless to try to follow the 15th when they were moving at full speed—especially into the middle of a pitched battle.

Angelo shook his head in resignation. "Then you'd better draw up papers on me, too, Lieutenant." He jumped to his tank, the *Trojan Horse,* ignoring her outcries.

Big shuttles and transport ships, tiny recon fliers, hangars, and repair gantries—they were all equal targets of the blue horde. And the defenders were becoming fewer and fewer.

Trying to see through the smoke in the cockpit of her damaged VT, Marie plunged toward the hardtop. She had become an ace and more in the course of the attack, but number six had *her* number, and got a piece of her just as she finished him.

She managed to throw the switches and do the imaging

that sent her VT into Guardian mode. It reconfigured just in time, foot thrusters blaring as it ground in for a stand-up landing.

As was often the case with Robotechnology, damage suffered in one mode was less critical in another, and the very act of mechamorphosis seemed to help the craft cope.

But she was no sooner at a standstill than enemy blasts gouged the runway all around her. The red Bioroid, like a stooping bird of prey, plunged at her. The Guardian's thrusters gushed, and she leapt it high.

Gotta take him out! They raced at each other, firing.

"I copy." Green turned from the phone to Emerson. "The airbase is putting up only scattered resistance, sir. It could fall at any time."

Emerson wondered what would happen if it did. Would the aliens try to annex it—set up ground operations? Or would they simply plunder what Protoculture they could find and torch the whole installation?

Leonard and the other higher-ups had been adamant that the Hovertanks be used to protect population centers rather than deployed to Fokker Base, where Emerson wanted them in the first place. But now the top brass were out of contact, communication virtually nil, and Emerson had room to use his *own* personal initiative.

"Bring in the Hovertanks. Get the fifteenth over there ASAP."

"Even 'as soon as possible' isn't soon enough, sir," Rochelle observed. "It'll take too long to get a message through and redeploy them."

"Try anyway!" Emerson snapped. Rochelle rushed to obey.

"Sir, shall I inform all units to be ready to evacuate the base?" Green hazarded the question. Emerson just stared at the tactical displays.

Marie and the red Bioroid played out their deadly game of high/low hide-and-seek as Bioroids and VTs clashed, fired, and were destroyed on all sides.

Marie's Guardian landed and glanced around the repair area in which it found itself, a big pulse laser gun held like a pistol in its cyclopean fist. "Okay, where y'at now?" she murmured.

She didn't have to wait long for a reply. The red came swooping over a building at her. The Guardian sprang up to meet it; as in a joust, they passed within arm's length of each other, firing away, dodging each other's fire.

But when Marie landed, the knees of her mecha gave way, cut in half by the red's energy shots. The Guardian crashed down on its chin, dazing her. She fought back the wooziness, popping the canopy and dragging herself out.

She pulled off her helmet and shoved it aside, then froze. The red had settled its Hovercraft right in front of her, and she was staring up the barrel of the discus-shaped pistol, a barrel as big as a storm drain. Marie watched, unmoving, waiting for the end.

But it wasn't the end either she *or* the red had expected. A cannon bolt came in, a thin one at high resolution set for long-distance work. The shot didn't quite take off the end of the Bioroid's arm; it missed by only a few feet.

Still, it threw up smoke and rubble, and appeared to stagger the red. Marie hugged the hardtop, shielding her head. Then she looked up, and saw where the shot had come from.

The 15th was lined up abreast and waiting. Dana stood up in her cockpit-turret, surveying her handiwork proudly as the red Bioroid pivoted to face her. She waved. "Over here, ya big metal dink! Can't ya even tell when somebody's *shooting* at you?"

As she hoped, the Bioroid rose on its platform, forgetting Marie, and rushed at her. Dana was back in her tank in a moment, the *Valkyrie* going through mechamorphosis to Gladiator, the rest of the 15th emulating her.

Dana's next salvo missed the red but knocked it waffling off course, nearly out of control. The rest of the ATACs were shooting at the blue Bioroids that surged in at them. The massed main batteries of the 15th skeeted alien after alien out of the sky; the air shimmered with heat waves at the vast forces unleashed. Thick smoke from the burning base and the exploded mecha billowed through the air. The squat, massive Gladiators volleyed and volleyed, picking off more invaders while keeping the rest at bay with their tremendous volume of fire.

The red Bioroid dropped from its platform to the ground, and was joined by a blue, to attack on foot.

"One on your right, Lieutenant!"

"I see him, Bowie!" Looking after each other was a habit they would never break, she guessed. That suited her.

The red popped up from behind a mound of fallen concrete to stitch the side of her Gladiator with a row of shots. Any other mecha in the Earth arsenal would have been severely damaged or blown to smithereens, but *Valkyrie* was scarcely touched. Dana traversed her gun barrel and whammed away again. The shot went wide, and the red and the blue came charging at the 15th's position.

The red seemed as big as Mount Everest. It and Dana fired at the same moment, near misses that rocked each other. "Bowie, cover me!"

"You got it!" Bowie drove the red back, firing with everything his tank, the *Diddy-Wa-Diddy*, had, even though the twin barrels of the secondary batteries scarcely scratched the Bioroid's hide. The rest of the 15th was busy maintaining the shield of AA fire; Dana went to Battloid mode, springing through the air to confront the red.

The two mecha catapulted through the air at each other. Dana protected herself from the enemy's hand-weapon shots with the thick curve of armor mounted along one arm like an ancient duelist's *targone*.

In the meantime she drew a bead with her own titanic battle rifle, the reconfigured tank-mode cannon. The shot pierced the red's left shoulder in a spatter of molten metal and oily black smoke, a mecha-wound that spewed sparks and shrapnel and tongues of flame. The red went reeling and flailing back through the air, hit the ground with a crash, and lay sprawled. Dana rushed at it, intending to rip loose the power couplings and tubes connected to the head area, to disable it completely.

But as Dana charged in, it resumed firing. Only the reflexes of a young professional in superb condition let her leap her Battloid out of the line of fire. The red jumped to cover and so did Dana; in another moment they were playing duck-and-shoot once more.

"Angie, lay cover for me, can you?"

"It's on the way!" The cannonade from the *Trojan*

Horse sent the red bounding in retreat; Dana's Battloid launched itself after.

"Gotcha now!" She fired on the fly, scoring another hit on the left shoulder as the red twisted and flipped to avoid. The alien landed awkwardly, nearly toppling. When it spun for another blast at her, she was ready.

Dana's rifle-cannon bolt blew the discus-shaped hand weapon right out of the red's fist; it stood unmoving, as if stunned.

Dana centered it in her sights. *The war's over for you, hosehead!* At last, Earth had a POW.

Just then the Bioroid was in motion again. Straight for her. *"Huh?"*

It strode directly at her weapon's muzzle. "What the—"

She fired again, a high-resolution beam that seared a hold right through it at the waistline. The red stumbled, regained balance, and charged her like an enormous defensive tackle.

Again the visions and strangely compelling images filled her. Was it because this was how she was to die? she wondered. The wash of emotion and disorientation paralyzed her where she would otherwise certainly have cut the foe in two with as many shots as it took.

Before she could shake off the trance, though, the red drop-kicked her Battloid. She shook off her stupefaction and her Battloid reached to grapple, but the red had already jumped high, its flying disc platform skimming in under it to bear it away into the air.

The alien fired at her with the weapons emplaced in the steering stem's pod; she barely rolled out of the way in time to avoid being hit. The red zipped past.

"That tears it!" The *Valkyrie* hurled itself into the air, mechamorphosing. It landed solidly on both feet, in Gladiator mode, main battery traversing, Dana's sight reticle searching. *Let's see how they like it when I clean house on their assault craft!*

She fired off a max-power round, recalling how Bowie's accidental shot of the day before had momentarily stopped the invaders. She aimed for it and hit the glassy blue dome on the upper side of its nose, presuming that to be the bridge; the shot shattered the dome and elicited a splash of secondary explosion, smoke, and flame.

The red tottered again, shaken by the bolt as much as the assault craft, and its emotionless tinted visor-face swung back for a look at Dana. She and the rest of the 15th opened up on the raiders with everything they had, primaries and secondaries hammering. Three more of the blues fell in the blaststorm, but the red and the rest wove through the fire to return to their smoking, listing ship.

The raiders dove aboard. The rust-red attack ship realigned, then dove upward out of sight at great speed, before the ATACs could bring weapons to bear on it.

Suddenly, a new Triumvirate
Dana, Nova, Marie,
Each zigzagging from her side toward
The center of the triskelion.

Mingtao, *Protoculture: Journey Beyond Mecha*

"**T**HE BIOROIDS WERE ALL TIED IN TO THE AS-
sault ship," Rochelle reported. "Signal Intelligence and
ground observers, sensors, and after-action reports all
agree," he added. "The Bioroids were forced to retreat
when Sterling got a round into the ship and disrupted
their command capability. At least we've got *some* idea
how to handle their mecha."

But it was obvious the enemy would be much more
careful next time. Emerson rubbed his face wearily, feeling the bristles and looking forward to some sleep. "At
least there's a *little* good news."

"Yessir. Um—" Rochelle broached a very delicate
subject. "About Lieutenant Sterling abandoning her post
and disobeying orders—what d'we do?"

Everyone knew Emerson was Bowie Grant's official
guardian and Dana's unofficial one, but that had never
made any difference as far as the young people's treat-

ment in the Southern Cross military. Emerson knew what he would do to *any* junior officer who had done what Dana had, and after a moment's hesitation conceded to himself that it was only just.

Dana was singing loudly and, as usual, badly off key. The shower spray came down at her steam-hot, and she massaged out bruises and sore muscles. She bit her lip once or twice, pausing in her song to fight back images of the red Bioroid.

Maybe those thoughts were some alien weapon? In any case, she mustn't fall prey to them again!

The battle had been bad enough, but there was also a row of sleepless nights ahead, repairing and running maintenance, getting in replacements and shuffling the TO&E and doing yet *more* training, to get the 15th combat-ready again in less time than it could possibly take.

There was a pounding at her bathroom door. She could hear Nova Satori's voice over the rushing water, "Just can the arias, Lieutenant, and get a move on."

Dana reluctantly left the shower, winding a towel around her, and emerged from the tiny bathroom cubicle in a cloud of steam. "What d'you think, Nova? Do I have a future in show business?"

The MP lieutenant sneered. "Sure, sweeping up after the circus parade. Now, hurry up; we're late."

Dana was perfectly content to dawdle; Nova refused to tell her where she was being taken, or why, but it seemed pretty plain. "Aw, take it easy! You'll have me back in your lockup soon enough!"

Nova was leaning against the wall with arms folded. She blurted out angrily, "The ceremony's already—" She stopped, saw that Dana had caught it, shrugged to herself, and went on. "I'm taking you to receive a promotion for valor.

"They're bumping you to first looie."

"Come in, Space Station Liberty! Space Station Liberty, Space Station Liberty, this is Earth Control, Earth Control, please acknowledge, over."

The transmission had been going out ever since the Masters appeared to begin their probings of Earthly defenses. The UEG and Southern Cross were certain that Liberty was still there in its Trojan Lagrangian point—Number Five—out near Luna's orbit. All indications were that the crew was still alive. In some way the scientists and engineers were still trying to understand, the Masters seemed to be watching everything on the spectrum out Liberty's way. An op would no sooner try a frequency than it was jammed, at least as far as Earth–Liberty links were concerned.

With the flagships' arrival in Earth orbit, even the relay telesats had gone dead, and in the wake of that first barrage from Captain Komodo, the satellites had been blasted from the sky. Earth-based commo lasers were useless, what with the distortion caused by the planet's atmosphere.

But the communications people doggedly kept trying. Radio Station Liberty, with its unique Robotech long-range commo gear, was Earth's only hope for eventual contact with the SDF-3 and Rick Hunter's expedition. More, Liberty's personnel were Human beings, cut off from their home planet; Earth must make every effort on their behalf. A rescue mission out to Liberty was impossible, though. Earth lacked the ships, equipment, and facilities to mount such an expedition in the foreseeable future, now that its main aerospace installation had been so badly ravaged by the Bioroids.

But a research team over in the encryption systems shop at Signal Security came up with a makeshift solution. Earth and Liberty could phase their equipment to jump frequencies, seemingly at random, from one to the next, in milliseconds, and get in brief communications on each one before the Masters could jam it. The result would be resumed communications with Liberty and, it was hoped, Moon Base survivors.

The only problem was, somebody had to get the word, and the meticulously worked out schedule of freq jumps, through to Liberty.

"Now, I'm not going to b-s you," the briefing officer said to the young unit commanders ranged around the big horseshoe table. "Getting a tight-beam commo laser up into orbit and punching through a signal to Liberty is going to be one hairy mission."

He looked around at the leaders from Cosmic Units, TASC, ATAC, and the rest. "Supreme Headquarters is calling for volunteers. Personally, I think it should be done by assignment, but there it is. So far, only Lieutenant Crystal of TASC has consented to go on this mission."

Dana knew very well whom he was waiting for. Along with the Black Lions, her 15th had the only real combat experience in dealing with enemy mecha, and the heavily armored Hovertanks were the most effective weapons Earth had. Like any soldier who had been around for a while, she knew that one of the basic rules of existence was never to volunteer. Still, a little something extra would be expected of the ATACs; she knew that when she applied for training, and so had everybody else in the 15th.

She swallowed and rose to her feet. "You can deal us in, sir." Marie lifted one eyebrow and gave Dana a half smile.

"Very commendable," the briefing officer nodded. "But we're going to have room for only three Hovers. You pick."

Dana got the point of what a critical assignment she had volunteered for when she discovered that the mission briefing was to be given by General Emerson himself.

He wasn't sweet, gruff Uncle Rolf then; he was all business and military precision. His only concession to their former relationship was when, shaking her hand— as he had Marie's and the others'—he gave her a short, minimal flash of smile and growled, "Good luck, Lieutenant Sterling; go get 'em."

She decided to take Angelo and Bowie. Bowie accepted it without any show of emotion, with barely a word of acknowledgment. Angelo had to put on an elaborate show, with a lot of talk about going head-on against an enemy armada single-handed, but Dana had confidence in him ever since he went along with her "personal initiative" decision to race to the rescue at Fokker Base.

The rest of the 15th showed some disappointment about being left behind, but kept it to themselves, even Sean. Dana reminded herself to be wary of the ATACs' own heartbreaker, but she was beginning to feel that she could rely on him, too.

Emerson and Green stood studying the image of the

enemy dreadnaught. "Are you sure Sterling and Crystal are qualified to command this mission, sir?" Green's voice echoed through the command center. "They do seem rather young for so much responsibility."

Emerson nodded thoughtfully. "Yes, but they're the best we have at leading our most powerful mecha, and they're the only two unit commanders alive who've engaged the Bioroids. And both did it effectively."

Emerson pursed his lips for a moment, then added ominously, "If anyone can do it, they can."

A command center captain named Anderson pointed out changes in the readouts; the enemy mother ship was in motion again. "They're moving into a lower orbit again, looks like."

All the launchpads for the real heavyweights were still out of commission. There were only two left that could accept shuttles, and so the mission was built around that limit; the launchpads were reusable, of course, but not in a short enough turnaround time to be of any help. Repair to damaged pads was going on around the clock, but that was of even less use today.

The two tiled white shuttles sat like delta-winged crossbow quarrels on the inclined launch ramps. Marie was in the pilot's seat in the number one ship, the *Challenger IV*; only a few hundred yards away sat the *Potemkin*.

Her copilot, Heideger, was an experienced captain from Cosmic Units. It was only over Cosmic's objections that a TASC officer had been given command, but Marie was glad to have Heideger as her first officer anyway; the man really knew his job.

They were completing the long preflight checklist. "We're now on internal computers," Heideger said. The flight deck door slid open and Dana and Bowie entered. They were unarmored, the expected g-load being what it was, and Dana carried—Marie couldn't believe her eyes —a *magazine*! As if this were some commuter hop!

"You're late," Marie bristled.

"We were securing the tanks—" Bowie began, taken aback.

"Stow it, Private, and get to your station!" Marie spat.

Now it was Dana's turn to bristle. "He was following my orders, *Lieutenant*. Or would you like a few dozen tons of Hovertank bouncing around during launch?"

Marie drew a deep breath. "Dana, zip your lip and siddown! We're already in pre-ignition."

Voices from launch control were talking to her and to Heideger. Marie turned back to her instrument panel and began tapping touchpad squares; Dana and Bowie got to their seats just as the main engines began firing up. All systems were green.

Dana sat at a station somewhat behind Heideger, fac- ing outboard, at the astrogation officer's station, which doubled as a gun position. In case of attack, her field of fire would protect the shuttle's port-midships area. Bowie was the next one aft, at the communications position, which also controlled the port-stern guns. Angelo Dante was at the starboard-midships guns, and a shuttle crew- man was across from Bowie at the starboard-stern guns.

Dana affected boredom with the final countdown pro- cedures. She had been on launches before, in training, and regarded them as overdramatized and unnecessarily complicated—just the sort of thing the Cosmic Units and the TASC types loved. Tankers believed in results, not ceremony! The whole thing brought out her rebellious streak.

Heideger swung around to take care of something else, punching up revised orbital ballistics, and saw that she had opened the fashion magazine on her lap. "Lieutenant, this isn't like ATACs; pay attention, because we *work* for a living around here, and everybody has to be alert!"

He turned back to his duties at once, and Marie, though she heard it, was too busy to give Dana a chewing out. Dana, as always, reacted to somebody else's orders with stubborn defiance. She opened the magazine and thumbed through the latest looks from around the world.

What d'you know; they were wearing empire-waisted, opaque stuff down in Rio, with metallic body-paint designs underneath—very daring. The rage in Osaka was all synthetic eelskin and lace. Micronesians were going in for beaded numbers with a total coverage about equivalent to a candy-bar wrapper!

The pre-ignition burn went on as the launchpads raised the shuttles up to their correct launch angle. All systems checked out. Marie found a moment in which to hope she hadn't done the wrong thing by not arguing against Dana's presence on the mission. *The kid's got guts, but she's bullheaded. And now she's 'zoided out with this magazine riff. I just hope she can keep her mind right upstairs the way she does on the ground.*

The shuttles came vertical as their primary engines flared and alpine mounds of rocket exhaust rose. At a precise moment the gantries released them, and the two ships lifted off, slowly at first, quickly gathering speed.

Dana felt herself pressed back deep into her acceleration seat.

Suddenly her magazine slipped from where she'd tucked it between her knees. It flopped open and pasted itself across her face like a determined starfish attacking a choice oyster. She struggled against it, her yells muffled by the magazine. *Has anything more embarrassing ever happened to me? Nope, can't think of any. . . .*

"Told ya," she dimly heard Heideger say in disgust. No one could help her; they were all weighted by the heavy g's. The best she could do was lever the magazine up and breath around the edges.

Suddenly a voice said, "This is the *Potemkin*, Lieutenant Borgnine speaking—Oh!"

She realized that his transmission had somehow been routed to her console as well as to Marie's and Heideger's. So, Borgnine was looking right at her. "Um, are you all right?"

"Just a second," Dana tried to say, but it came out, "Mnff uh ff-uh." Meanwhile, at the end of an eternity, the engine burn was over, and she felt a moment's zero-g as the shuttle's artificial gravity cut in.

Dana lowered the magazine, blood rushing back into her white face in a furious blush. She had a feeling she was in for some black and blue from her close encounter with haute couture.

"I'm fine!" she tried to say brightly.

Borgnine's copilot, who looked about thirteen years old, leaned over to inform his boss, "Computers say we're coming up for a new course correction."

Borgnine frowned. "What? That's much too soon. Marie, what d'your internal computers show?"

"We'll check it out and get right back to you," she said. Ideally, they would have bucked the problem back to Earth, but the Masters' interference had already put them beyond communication range.

Marie took time out to chuckle, "Hey, Dana! How'd that facial feel?"

Both shuttles jettisoned the spent solid-fuel boosters as the crews worked to find out why Borgnine's computer was acting up. The *Potemkin*'s autopilot seemed adamant that a course correction was needed, and the overrides didn't seem to be dissuading it.

"I have more bad news," Bowie said quietly. "The invaders are comin' our way. Only this time there are two of them, two mother ships."

CHAPTER
ELEVEN

At this moment my hand is bleeding; I crushed a glass in frustration because I can't find out what is going on up there— none of us can! And yet I can tell something has happened to Dana, is happening to her, by means that are my secret to guard.

Ah, the Protoculture, it demands so much in return for revealing its mysteries! My life is a tiny price to pay. And Dana's, even less.

Dr. Lazlo Zand, notes for *Event Horizon: Perspectives on Dana Sterling and the Second Robotech War*

MARIE TURNED TO BOWIE. "HOW SOON CAN WE get that transmission off?"

Bowie, who was responsible for making the actual transmission, did not think things looked very good. "I'm not picking up anything from them yet, Lieutenant." And the laser hadn't even been deployed yet. It was a very tight one, for the long shot to Liberty; it had been presumed that it would take some time to establish contact, and there didn't seem to be much of that.

"Hurry it up; we've got company coming," Marie said, and went back to her flying.

Borgnine's shuttle carried no special apparatus; it was an escort ship. Moreover, there was little he could do to help anybody now, with his computers leading a life of their own. And all the time, the alien leviathans closed in on the shuttles.

Then, despite anything Borgnine and his crew could do, his engines fired. "Cut your engines! Retrofire!" Marie hollered into her mike. It did no good; *Potemkin* accelerated, directly toward the Masters' monolith that loomed on its vector.

No one could tell whether what was happening was some explainable glitch—some damage done during the Bioroids attack, perhaps, and not detected—or something the Robotech Masters had instigated. It didn't matter; the shuttle blazed toward the invader like an interceptor missile.

Borgnine tried everything he could think of, to no effect. Engines would not shut down, retros wouldn't fire, computers wouldn't listen, and altitude jets were insistently silent.

"C'mon, girl, steady. Steady now," Borgnine implored his ship.

A separate warning system computer flashed red lights and alarm whoopers, saying in its emotionless female voice, "Danger, danger. Collision alert. Collision is imminent, repeat, imminent."

"Lieutenant Crystal, I've got a runaway here," he told Marie. "Nothing we can do." Still, they tried everything they could think of.

An invader ship—the Robotech Masters' flagship—grew huge before them as they bore down on it. "Be informed: this might be enemy-induced. You're on your own. Good lu—" The shuttle slammed into the alien supership at max velocity; the impact and the detonating weapons, fuel and power systems, made an explosion that lit the faces of Marie and her copilot hundreds of miles away.

Marie instinctively put in a transmission to Earth, to inform them of the *Potemkin*'s death, just in case they were receiving down below.

Dana stood frozen by the sudden destruction of so many men and women, hearing Borgnine's last words. *You're on your own.*

"Why . . . why couldn't we . . . help them . . ."

But even more than the shock of the crash, she was frozen by this first close look at the alien flagship. It, too, seemed a remembered thing from an impossible recollection. Superimposed on it was the blank, enigmatic vision of the red Bioroid.

She sat trembling like a leaf at her station, only partially hearing Marie's biting reply. "Nothing we *could* do, you know that. We're all volunteers, remember? To tell you the truth, Lieutenant, I expected better of you. Now, shut up and do your job!"

"Enemy's now at eight hundred miles and closing fast," Heideger said matter-of-factly. There was no point in trying to outrun the swift aliens, and besides, *Challenger IV* had a mission to perform.

"*Potemkin* appears to have been destroyed, sir," the announcement came in the command center.

"What about *Challenger IV*?" an operations officer asked.

"Information limited due to enemy jamming, but the mother ships appear to be closing on the remaining shuttle."

* * *

At a distance of four hundred miles, the flagship launched assault boats. Bowie still had no contact with Space Station Liberty.

"Lieutenant, take over fire control," Marie ordered.

But Dana could only sit, trembling, eyes frozen on her instruments and the pistol-grip fire control. Before her were overlapping images of the alien ship, of the assault craft, and the Bioroid—every moment of her combats against it came back in overwhelming detail, shutting out all other thought. And on the periphery of her awareness were emotions to which she could put no name.

Bowie looked at her worriedly, but there was no time to stop to find out what was wrong. "I show enemy craft at one hundred miles and closing."

Angelo had swung around in his acceleration chair. "Lieutenant, she said 'take command.' Dana? C'mon, snap out of it!"

"Save it, Sergeant," Marie cut him off. "I'll take fire control. Gunners select targets and fire as soon as they're within range."

The assault ships started pitching at longer range than that of the shuttle's guns, but soon the two forces were sufficiently close to each other for both to be throwing out everything they had. The shuttle had a defensive shield that protected it from immediate damage, but the shield couldn't last long under the pounding it was taking.

Marie, Angelo, and the others bent to their guns—all except Dana. The firing controls were standard Robotech setups, as familiar to the ATACs troopers as to the TASC pilot.

The assault craft spread out. "They're trying to surround us!" Marie called as the twin-barreled gun mounts swung and threw out torrents of flaring disc bolts, the enemy answering with the same. "Take evasive action," she added to Heideger.

"Trying, Lieutenant," he said evenly, but the wallowing shuttle was no match for the attackers.

"Sir, enemy vessels are surrounding *Challenger*," a command center officer relayed the news.

"Has it been hit?"

Nova Satori, watching the displays at Colonel Fredericks's side, dreaded the answer. She might have little use for Dana's and Marie's lack of discipline, but Nova was behind them one hundred percent right now, and rooting silently.

"Heavy activity out there, sir, and we're still not getting reliable sensor readings—we can't be sure."

Nova watched the screens and waited.

"One coming your way, Sergeant!" Marie yelled.

"I see 'im," Angelo said distractedly, poised over his scope and pistol-grip control stick. He led his target and got it dead center; it vanished in a cloud of superheated gas.

"Good shooting!" Marie called. At that moment another bandit drilled a line of holes along the shuttle's port side.

"Shields failing," Heideger said. "Still no contact with Liberty or ground control." Another close one shook the spacecraft.

Marie realized abruptly that Dana wasn't firing. "Sterling, what's the matter with you?" A quick look told her

Dana wasn't hurt. "Come on, defend your sector! We need you!"

Got to . . . get hold of myself, Dana kept repeating as if it were an incantation. But she couldn't move, hypnotized by the visions assailing her. By sheer force of will she compelled herself to say, "Yeah. I'm okay."

All at once her trance turned to an all-engulfing fear. *I shouldn't be here! I can't handle this! I'll let everyone down!*

Marie was up, to swing Dana's chair around and slap her hard across the face. "Snap out of it! Stop acting like a coward!"

Dana sat, dazed. Marie turned to Heideger. "Get someone else up here to man these guns!" She jumped back for the pilot's seat.

Dana was staring at the firing control as if she had never seen one before, and another energy disc impact sent the shuttle lurching. "Missed him!" Angelo yelled. "Dana, he's coming around to your side."

More were doing the same; the aliens had realized that Dana's sector was a vulnerable point.

The lurch had thrown Dana against the fire-control grip, and she clung to it by reflex. She instinctively thumbed the trigger button over and over. The assault craft broke off its attack run as her fire nearly nailed it.

"It's nice to have ya back." She heard Angelo's grin in his tone as she fought to center the gunsight reticle on the assault craft.

What was I doing? I could've gotten us all killed! But she thrust the thought aside as the bogie came around for another pass. The reticle centered. *Your time's up, chump!*

She thumbed the trigger again and again. The assault boat suddenly wobbled off course, leaking flame, and explosive decompression turned the leak into a brief *whoosh*, like a blowtorch. The crippled invader disappeared beneath the shuttle.

More enemy ships had been coming in at Dana's field of fire, and thinking it a soft spot, crowded together. She picked off another, and damaged a third as they sought frantically to evade.

"Good shooting, Lieutenant," Angelo admitted.

Heideger got the shuttle back under control and stabilized the damage while the others tried to drive back the assault ships and Bowie made desperate efforts to get a bearing on Liberty.

"I think the only way we're gonna do it is to get the shuttle back on a steady course," he said.

"We're closing with the mother ship," Marie informed them. There wasn't much hope of evading. "Everybody get ready."

Dana waited at her station; it had been a good try, a good try. . . . A gallant final fight.

She wondered where the targets had gone. Then Heideger called out, "The assault ships are withdrawing. They appear to be breaking off the attack."

The shuttle's guns went silent and the crew sat stunned, not believing that they were still alive. "I don't get it," Dana blinked. Nobody else did either.

But Angelo reported, "I'm picking up a directed force field on the mother ship. I think it's a charged particle beam projector."

Suddenly, enormous hyphens of energy were blazing all around them, monster discharges like nothing the

Humans had ever seen before. But it seemed the mega-volleys were so enormously powerful that they were far less accurate than the flagship's other weapons.

Or maybe they're just playing with us again, it occurred to Marie. *We'll know in a few seconds.* She hit the ship's thrusters, accelerating as quickly as she dared—straight for the flagship. "Now, if we can just get in under it before it gets us!"

The bright comets of the Masters' superweapon cascaded around the shuttle as Marie wove and sideslipped with all the skill at her command. There were shouts and objections from everybody else on the flight deck.

"There's no such thing as 'out of range' to that particle gun!" Marie cried. "We'll have to get in close, where it can't get a fix on us!" The shuttle shook and seemed to want to come apart. "Brace yourselves!"

The *Challenger IV* dove in at the flagship, homing in under its vast belly. Far above, they could make out something like an enormous fish-eye lens between the hyphens of destruction it spewed forth. Then all at once the shuttle was in an area of peace and quiet, out of the megaweapon's field of fire. The Bioroids, of course, had pulled way back once that big Sunday punch let loose. The shuttle was zooming along all alone.

"Nice move, Lieutenant," Angelo conceded.

She headed in under the gargantuan ship's belly, weaving in and out of the superstructural features. "This is just a breather! There are still those AA cannon that got the Redhawks." And, they all knew, the Bioroids probably hadn't exactly headed home for the locker rooms, either.

Marie shed most of her speed with a retro-burn, steering with extremely wasteful thruster blasts that couldn't be avoided. The shuttle zipped along with the mother ship's underbelly only a few dozen yards overhead. It wove between a stupendous grotto of the insectile communications spars, like a cruise through some eerie undersea city. It passed among upside-down tuning-forklike things as big as high-rises, and downhanging Towers of Babel.

"Looks clear through there, Lieutenant," Heideger said, pointing.

Angelo forgot to breathe for a while, looking around him at the screens, the viewports. The briefings hadn't done the vessel justice. "This thing's gigantic," he understated.

Marie nodded to herself as she wended the ship along. She murmured, "I—I've never seen anything like it. . . ." It felt more like being in a submarine than a spacecraft.

"Say again, Lieutenant?" Dana piped up.

Marie turned a scathing look on her. "Paying complete inattention to practically everything today, are we, *Lieutenant*?"

Dana looked contrite. Marie glanced beyond her. "Hey, Bowie! Any luck getting a beam through?"

Bowie worked away. "Not a chance. No line of sight. Besides, all these electronic echoes and all this energy clutter are frying the avionics."

"Any word yet, young man?" Commodore Tessel called in the command center.

A tech replied crisply, "Well, sir, we're showing *something* on the sensors, but we aren't sure what it is. We're getting sloppy images, and the interpretation computers can't sort them out."

Sean Phillips and Louie Nichols entered the command center. Nobody had invited them, but Emerson noted their entrance, did not object, and his subordinates let things stand as they were. "Anything from the *Challenger*?" Sean asked Nova Satori quietly, anxiously.

The command center was a restricted area; she had no idea what favors were called in or Phillips's wiles had been used to gain entry, but Nova knew she should be chasing the two ATACs troopers out.

It just didn't seem right, though, with so many dead and so many more, perhaps, about to die. "We're getting distorted signals, so we're not sure what's happening," she told Sean.

"There," the tech said just then. "I think that's them! But—the reason our signal's distorted is because they're so close to one of the enemy mother ships. "Hell's own bells! It's right on top of them!"

The shuttle was barely drifting along. "Staying tight as possible," Marie said, tight-lipped.

"Creepy silences. *Man*, I hate creepy silences," Dana muttered.

"I suppose you'd rather have them shooting at us again?" Angelo shot back.

"Don't worry, ground-pounders!" Marie said tartly. "There'll be lots more shooting, and soon." The three ATACs frowned at that; they were armored troopers, not leg infantry ground-pounders.

Marie hunched forward in her chair; the shuttle was coming to the end of the flagship's underbelly. "Get ready to try for contact again."

"Ready and waiting," Bowie said evenly.

"Everybody look sharp," Marie said. "I'm taking us up for a look-see."

She hit the main thrusters and zoomed up from underneath the immense flagship. Immediately, two of the chandelier-bulb cannon swung into place and sent out tangled vines of green-white destruction.

"Oh, *now* they manage to find us, now that we're not hiding." Marie laughed scornfully, taking the shuttle through evasive maneuvers. "On your toes, all of you! We'll be getting company!" Still, the fact that the enemy seemed to have lost track of the *Challenger* once the shuttle was close in underneath was not to be forgotten.

"Alien assault ship on our tail," Angelo called out.

"And I'm picking up two more coming in on our flanks," Dana added.

But the alien ships refrained from firing this time. There was still more that the Robotech Masters wished to know about these primitive Earthlings, creatures like missing links really, who had in some unfathomable manner wiped out the giant Zentraedi.

The launch bays of the assault ships opened, and Bioroids zoomed forth.

Marie had partial shields back, but she zoomed in low to the flagship's upper hull, skimming it, so that the enemy cannon couldn't be depressed low enough to hit the shuttle.

The Bioroids, on the other hand, had trouble getting a clear shot, swarming as thickly as they did; they ran the risk of hitting their own ship or one another.

"Bowie, resume contact-scan," Marie ordered.

"Roger; scanning," Bowie responded. The laser-contact with Liberty required enormous precision. That would mean that *Challenger IV* was going to have to do less maneuvering, at least for a little while. And that in turn meant that somebody was going to have to keep the Bioroids away from the shuttle; repel them perhaps, or better yet, decoy them.

"Take over," Marie told Heideger. "I'm going to suit up." She began making her way to the rear cargo bay, and her Veritech.

CHAPTER
TWELVE

You can't get somebody in your sights in combat without spending a lot of time after that wondering if you're in somebody else's.

Remark made by Dana Sterling to Nova Satori

THE BIOROIDS BEGAN TO PRESS THEIR ATTACK; Heideger threw in some jukes-and-jinxes as the top cargo bay doors opened to make Marie's launch less of a clay-pigeon shoot.

The VT roared out into the dark vacuum, and most of the Bioroids turned to pursue at once, leaving the others to dodge the shuttle's fire. Dana and Angelo each managed to flame a blue enemy mecha.

Then it was again all turns-and-burns for Marie, a furious dogfight in the uncaring void. She bagged three of them in harrowing, furious maneuvering much more appropriate to atmospheric fighting than airless space; Robotech craft moved very much in accordance with the pilot's imaging, and Marie was much more comfortable flying where aerodynamics and control surfaces counted.

Then a fourth alien foe got a line of shots into her fuselage, but only at a grazing angle, so that they did little damage. She turned on the blue vengefully, flamed it, and neatly avoided fire from two more.

Suddenly a shape from her nightmares swooped close, the red Bioroid aiming for her. "Oh, no, you don't!" She hit emergency power, blasting away, at the same time putting the VT through mechamorphosis. The VT reconfigured to Guardian mode. Marie was about to come around for another go at the red, but two blues pounced on her before she could.

Inside the shuttle, Heideger yelled, "Marie's in trouble!"

Dana waxed another blue but missed the one behind it. "Look, we've all got our own problems. Bowie, talk to me."

Bowie was intent at his work at the commo suite. "Tentative contact. I think I've got a fix on them."

"Raise the laser-transmitter," Dana ordered; that would risk having it damaged, but there wasn't much time left, and the volunteers would just have to gamble.

Outside, Marie led the first blue along, getting it between her and the second, then zapping it thoroughly. The second came through the spherical fireball of the first, blinded a bit by it, so that she took it by surprise and peppered it with a sustained burst. It, too, was obliterated.

"Transmitter in position," Bowie said over the tactical net.

Marie spared a quick glance while maneuvering and craning for more opponents. "Roger! I see it!" The laser had emerged from an armored pod over the flight deck. It was such a fragile, unimpressive-looking device, it occurred to Marie, to have been the centerpiece of such carnage.

A blue seemed to notice the apparatus and go in for a shot at it, but Marie pounced on it from the six o'clock position and shot the alien war machine to shreds.

"Awright, Bowie, now or never," Dana said, swinging her guns to a new target.

Bowie began sending the encoded transmission in burst format; all the information was contained in a single micro-pulse that was repeated over and over. If just one pulse got through, the Liberty operators could decrypt it instantly, reprogram their transmitters, and resume contact. The pulse-message also detailed what had happened on Earth since the aliens' appearance.

The problem was that the shuttle was being battered so badly by enemy fire that not even the complex compensating gear could keep the beam well on target.

The shuttle volunteers began firing again, pressing the triggers until their thumbs grew tired, as more Bioroids came in at them to replace the ones they destroyed. Marie turned and was a split-second too late to dodge, and the red Bioroid came at her out of nowhere and scored a hit. She twisted the Guardian to avoid the worst of the blast, and smashed against the shuttle's fuselage. "I'm hit!"

"Marie!" Dana yelled over the net.

"It's that red Bioroid," Marie moaned in pain as the marauder came at her in another pass. Her Guardian barely got out of the way, but the red gave an impression of toying with her. "He's too quick for me!"

Dana looked at the scene on the external monitors,

wide-eyed. *It's the same one*, she knew with a certainty she never questioned. *The one I—I'm afraid of. But why? What are these strange feelings? And now it's going to kill Marie.*

But a diamond-hard resolve came into her. *No! I won't let it!* "I'm going out there," she decided, rising from her place.

Bowie and Angelo started to object, but she was already dashing aft. "Do your best to hold them. And get that message through!"

The endless drill of the Academy and duty with the 15th served her well; in seconds she was in armor, climbing into her Battloid-mode mecha. *I know how that Bioroid thinks! I don't know how, but I do! I can beat him!*

"More bandits coming," Angelo reported as the cargo bay doors opened again. The doors swung up and out to reveal a volume of space filled with the deadly blossoms of explosions and the streaming discs of the Robotech energy weapons.

A blue saw the opening and tried to ride its Hovercraft right down into the shuttle cargo bay. Dana's Battloid brought up its heavy rifle and hosed the blue with blazing energy, sending it back in burst fragments.

She swung the rifle back and forth, driving back nearby attackers. "Hang on, Marie! I'll be right with you!"

"Thanks," Marie said, sounding harried. "I could use the help."

"Bowie! Any response from Liberty?"

Sweat ran down Bowie's face in rivulets. "Not yet."

* * *

Tessel tried to contain his frustration. "Why hasn't Liberty answered? Why?"

Like everyone else in the command center, he was afraid what the answer might be. Perhaps the whole theory behind the plan was wrong, or the equipment wasn't up to the job. Or perhaps there was no one alive at Space Station Liberty to hear.

"Sir, we can't raise Liberty *or* the shuttle. It's beginning to look like it's a wipe, sir," a G2 analyst reported.

Nova heard the sharp intake of breath at her side, Sean and Louie. The three young soldiers said nothing, fearing it might bring bad luck; they watched the screens, not blinking, not moving.

Dana added the tremendous firepower of her Battloid to that of Marie's Guardian and the shuttle's batteries. Heideger somehow kept minimal shield power, although the ship took a number of hits. The whole area around the shuttle was a crisscrossing of the heaviest firing Dana had ever seen. Bioroids came apart in mid-pounce, only to be replaced by more.

Then Marie called out, "You can't win! You're not even *Human*!" and Dana saw that the red had reappeared like a Horseman of the Apocalypse, diving at the Black Lion leader. Marie and the red chopped away at each other with intense fire until the range was very short, nearly point-blank. Then the red sheered off and came around for another try.

"Dana, he's headed your way! I'm joining you!"

In moments, Marie was in the bay beside Dana, shoulder to shoulder, muzzles aimed high as the enemy leader rushed in at them again, his oval hand weapon putting out rounds one on top of the next.

It became a collision course, the two women and the alien vying to see which side could put out a more murderous volume of fire. VT Battloid and Hovertank Battloid stood their ground as the red closed in.

"Just keep shooting, Dana, keep shooting!"

Bolts from the heavy cannon that was Dana's rifle scored at last, ripping into the edge of the red's visor, so that smoke and burning scrap spun from it. The red veered off yet again, to regain balance.

"Don't stop! He can't last long!" Marie said as the red came in at them on a new track. "You've got the angle; he's yours!"

Dana's Battloid spread its feet and stood like a metal titan flinging starflame. The red came in, and, as if events had become snarled in some kind of chrono-dimensional loop, she scored a sustained shot on the same part of the left shoulder she'd hit in the fight at Fokker Base. Once more the shoulder nearly separated; once more the red tumbled away like a seared and flailing Lucifer cast down.

Dana's mind reeled. Was this past, present, future? Was it real? "I—I got him!" she cried, bringing herself out of the disorientation.

"Good shooting, ground-pounder." Marie laughed. As before, the blue Bioroids broke off their attack as soon as their leader withdrew from the field of battle.

Inside the shuttle, Bowie activated the new frequency-jumping commo system, patching an incoming message through the tactical net so that Dana and Marie could hear it. "This is Space Station Liberty calling Earth, Space Station Liberty calling Earth. Do you copy? We have relayed your message to Moon Base. Repeat, Moon Base has resumed contact as well."

Bowie and Angelo were up, pounding each other on the back. They were about to drag Heideger into it when they saw that he was slumped, lifeless, in the copilot's seat. The joy ebbed from them.

"Oh, no . . ." Heideger had taken a fatal charge from an energy surge during the final attack. Angelo, nearly in tears, closed the man's eyes for the last time.

"They made it! Mission accomplished! *Challenger*'s heading home!" a command center tech whooped. Sean and Louie stood watching the place turn into a madhouse of celebration. Even Nova Satori was smiling, eyes shining.

Louie adjusted his dark goggles and shrugged to Sean. "With three ATACs up there—what'd they expect?"

High above the Earth, in the flagship of the Robotech Masters, all aspects of the encounter were reexamined and subjected to a coldly merciless scrutiny. The Scientist clone triumvirate had primary responsibility in this matter, though, of course, the Politician triumvirate was working in close coordination—a coordination difficult for the uncloned to imagine.

Silent discussions and debates took place, moderated through the Master triumvirate's humped Protoculture cap. The many mental voices spoke in the precision of artificially induced psi contact; they were unhampered by any emotion.

It was clear that the space station and the lunar base were in contact with the primitives below once more, in a fashion that thwarted, for the time being, the Masters' ability to jam. The humans had millions upon millions of frequencies among which to jump, and even the resources of the Robotech Masters were finite—the more so now that Protoculture was in such short supply.

Resumed communication was of little moment, though, and the losses in Bioroids and assault ships was of scant concern. It was the *un*known that troubled the Masters. Thus far, there had been no sign of the enigmatic weapons or powers that had destroyed most of the Zentraedi race, and some five million warships.

Certainly, there had been no use of any such thing as yet. Still, though the Masters were arrogant and supremely egotistical—despite their decadence, and the blind eye they turned to their own decline—they harbored no illusions when it came to recognizing the power of giant cloned warriors they had created. Whatever had defeated the Zentraedi—had virtually swallowed the countless goliaths and their fleets and mecha like some black hole—was a force to be feared even by the Robotech Masters.

Perhaps all that had gone before was a clever Human ruse, it occurred to the cold intellects in the flagship. Perhaps all of this sacrifice and seeming vulnerability on the part of the primitives was a strategy to draw the Masters on until they met the fate of the Zentraedi.

Another body of opinion had it that whatever force had obliterated the Zentraedi—and there was evidence that that force might have been the Zentraedi themselves —it no longer existed. Therefore: press ahead; strike for the treasure beyond treasures that lay below.

And overhanging all debate was the need, the hunger,

for Protoculture. Though the Masters would never have framed it so, without Zor's greatest creation they were a dying race of refugees; however, with it they would be, as they thought of themselves, Lords of all Creation.

The longing and need was greater than any mortal could ever conceive; a vampire's thirst was a mere dryness of the throat by comparison. A decision was reached in the wake of the battle; the next phase of the Robotech Masters' plan was set into motion.

CHAPTER
THIRTEEN

Of course, Dana Sterling wasn't physically isolated in her upbringing; indeed, it was somewhat rough-and-tumble at times. But, while there are indications that she was not a virgin by the time she graduated from the Academy, she seemed to have formed no strong sexual bond of any kind—as if something were saving her as surely as Rapunzel being kept in a tower.

I refer the reader to the writings of Zand, Zeitgeist, and the rest as to what that something was; it seems certain that the events at the mounds and thereafter bear them out.

Altaira Heimel, *Butterflies in Winter; Human Relations and the Robotech Wars*

TWO HOVERCYCLES HOWLED THROUGH THE NIGHT side by side.

Dana knew there would be road grit and dust from the cinders of the wounded Earth to wash from her hair later, but she didn't care. Their headlights threw out cones of harsh light across the desolation as she and Bowie barreled across the wasteland.

A night patrol would ordinarily have been a crashing bore. It was a little like guarding the Gobi Desert; who was going to steal *this* piece of real estate? But the Southern Cross Army was on yellow alert in the wake of the *Challenger* ruckus, and everyone who wasn't grabbing some much-needed sleep was on ready-reaction standby. Heel-and-toe watches in the 15th's ready-room had just about driven Dana crazy, so she had jumped at the chance to take this patrol, to get away from the base for a while. Bowie had naturally come along, loyal and concerned as any brother.

Besides, there was a chance, however remote, that the Robotech Masters might try an invasion, which gave the joyride a little added voltage.

Her hair was only partly confined by the band of her goggles and the techno-ornament hairband she wore; Dana reveled in the whipping of the thick, short blond waves, and the feel of the wind in her face.

When the base signaled, she let Bowie handle it; she was enjoying herself too much. Then reality caught up with her.

Bowie cut in even nearer, until they were knee-and-knee at sixty miles an hour. Both slowed a bit, so they could talk rather than use their commo link; Bowie knew Dana hated to have the base eavesdropping.

"Headquarters has been tracking us!" Bowie yelled it slowly, so that she could read his lips—lit by his instrument panel lights and the backwash from the headlight— as well as strain to hear. "They said to come about, right now!"

They both took a low hummock of sand hardened into glass by a long-ago Zentraedi blast, like a pair of steeple-chasers. Dana nodded to him. "Okay, let's go." She'd learned early in life that freedom never lasted for long.

But as they swung around, their headlights scaring up rabbits and strange radiation-bred things that had come out in the darkness, sending them scuttling for cover, Dana exclaimed in surprise, then yelled, "Hold it!"

Both cycles retroed, then came to a halt, engines at low idle. *"Hmmm."*

Bowie saw that Dana was gazing off into the distance and looked that way. "Hey!" he yelped.

Searchlights, or at least what looked like searchlights, quartered the sky over in the east. In an earlier generation someone might have said it looked like a supermarket opening.

Dana shifted her bubble goggles up onto her forehead for a better look. "That sector's been totally off limits for as long as I can remember," she pondered. Someplace over there was the decaying vessel that had at last destroyed Macross City, and the mounds in which the Human race had entombed the remains of the SDF-1, SDF-2, and the flagship of Khyron the Backstabber, the mad Zentraedi battlelord.

Entombed there, too, was whatever remained of Bowie's aunt Claudia, Admiral Henry Gloval, and the three young women whose pictures Dana's godfathers had virtually worshipped all their lives.

Bowie was poised on the balls of his feet, straddling the cycle, which bobbed gently on its surface-effect thrusters, engine humming. "Lieutenant, I dunno. And I'm not eager to find out, either." He had seen the mounds from afar, many times, but something about them made him queasy, troubled.

She had been thinking along just the opposite line, he knew; Dana turned a vexed look on him. "Say again?"

"Just a joke! Just for grins!" he fended her off.

"Not funny, Private, got me?"

"Awright! Okay!" But he saw that the squall was past. She was looking at those lights again. "What d'we do now?" he asked, as if he didn't have a sinking feeling what the answer would be.

They were the strangest mecha, or robots, or machines, or whatever they were, that Dana had ever seen. There were a dozen of them or more, like big walking searchlights the size of a Gladiator, only the round lenses had been narrowed down like a cat's iris until they were thin slits. And the slits were rotating, so there were narrow fans of light reaching into the sky, seemingly thick, then thin, then thick again when seen from one side. The rays swept back and forth across the giant cairn of the fallen SDF-1, some occasionally sweeping past, to throw up the skybeams Dana and Bowie had spotted.

Dana couldn't make head or tail of the two-legged searchlights stumping back and forth or standing in ranks and seeming to irradiate the mound, but there was something else there that she did, and it almost made her heart stop.

The voice sounded reedy and distorted, like a Human voice heard by single-sideband transmission: artificial somehow, and quavering. "There can be no mistake," the red Bioroid said. "The creatures of this planet have attempted to disguise the Protoculture with a radioactive substance."

The alien mecha paced around the work area, fifty yards below, holding a strange circular instrument or tool in one mighty armored fist. At the time, Dana didn't question how she and Bowie heard and understood the words; it seemed that they were being amplified over a PA system.

"You will notify the mother ship that our calculations

were correct," the red went on to a rank of three blues who stood at attention. "We will make further preparations to excavate."

But the red knew it wouldn't be as simple as that, and that the effort to regain the Matrix faced opposition more serious than mere human interference. The three inorganic entities, the Protoculture wraiths the Masters had detected upon their arrival, had made their presence felt. Somehow, the guardians of the mounds were resisting the Bioroids' efforts to get a precise fix on exactly where the Matrix was, meaning that excavation using the Masters' unsubtle techniques ran the risk of damaging or even destroying the last existing means of Protoculture production.

More, the wraiths exuded an air of arctic-cold confidence, an aura that the Plan, the great Vision, of the original Zor would not be derailed. The wraiths were shaped by the Protoculture, of course; even the Robotech Masters must proceed with caution.

Yet the wraiths had evinced no physical or PSI powers beyond that of a small confusion of the Bioroids' instruments. The red Bioroid could think of two ways to proceed: a gradual, almost surgical exhumation, or a brute scooping-up of the entire area of the mounds and everything around them for later dissection. Neither process could be undertaken while the local primitives were still capable of mounting resistance; that would risk destruction of the Matrix with a stray missile, energy barrage— any of a number of awful possibilities.

The red Bioroid awaited the Masters' commands while the trio of black apparitions within the mounds, created by the Matrix for its own purposes, following the instructions and the Vision of Zor, gloated, and mocked the Robotech Masters.

From the top of the cliff overlooking the invader operation, Dana and Bowie looked down with cold coursings of despair rippling through them. An enemy vessel larger than an assault ship, looking somehow industrial, utilitarian, hung with its lower hull a mere few dozen yards off the ground. Other Bioroids were moving heavy equipment around on pallets and sledges that never touched the Earth.

How could they have gotten past our sensors? Dana thought with a sinking feeling. *Earth is wide open to them!* She simply stored the references about Protoculture and excavation for her after-mission report; the intel analysts would have to deal with all that.

She and Bowie were lying on their stomachs, peering down at the demons'-foundry scene of the Bioroid mining. Dana debated between the urge to report this catastrophic alien beachhead at once and the awareness that every scrap of intelligence could be of pivotal importance —that another few moments of eavesdropping might yield the key to the whole war.

Training and textbook procedures won out for once. She had vital information to get back to headquarters; follow-up would be somebody else's problem. She reached out to give Bowie a silent, all-but-invisible contact signal, a code of grip-and-finger-pressure that would tell him it was time to leave the area quietly, then run like hell.

That was when the red Bioroid, halting, turned its lustrous blue-black faceplate up in the Humans' direction.

Dana heard the words as clearly as if the stylized ornament in her hair were a real earphone: *I sense an enemy
presence.*

The blues were alert at once. The red turned ponder-
ously and stalked through the din and strobing of the
work area, the great head craning to look up at their hiding place. "Geddown! Freeze!" Dana whispered, doing
the same. They heard the resounding metal tread stop
near the base of the cliff. *It seemed to emanate from this
area,* the mind-voice said. *It would be advisable to have a
look.*

A flood of light came from below. Against all training
and every instinct save curiosity, Dana was moved by
those same mysterious impulses to peer over the cliff's
edge.

Bowie whispered, "What's goin' on, Lieutenant?" but
she simply couldn't answer, transfixed by what she saw.
Bowie eased up for a peek too. He saw that Dana was
transfixed, in some kind of daze.

The red Bioroid had halted and opened, its chest plas-
tron swinging forward, pieces of the shoulder pauldrons
and its helmet beaver swinging away, like an exploded
illustration in a tech manual. Nestled within was a glowing orb, like a gunner's ball-turret, with a metal framing
like lines of latitude and longitude, giving out a radiance
even more intense than the searchlights'. The light from
the orb grew brighter and brighter, then shot out long
lines of shadow as something moved in its very heart. A
tall, long-legged form emerged from the center of the un-
bearable incandescence.

The Human race had been working on the assumption
that these new invaders were like the Zentraedi, ten times

larger than Human stature, and that the metal things the Earth was fighting were basically offworld giants in armor. That obviously wasn't true, and Bowie didn't know what to expect now. He was thinking along the lines of revolting, icky critters, when a young demigod stepped out to stand with one booted foot up on the edge of the open chestplate, surveying everything around him with an air of supreme hauteur.

The creature seemed to be male, and looked Human enough, though with an elfin air and long eyes and ears. The face was a chiseled archetype, ageless and slender, handsome as a Grecian statue. Masses of lavender ringlets tumbled around the being's head and shoulders. The limbs were long, too, but muscled and graceful; the torso was slender but powerful and well defined in the tight, shiny black costume the Bioroid pilot wore.

The outfit had a military look to it, with high, open collar, broad yellow belt, and scarlet demisleeves covering the forearms. At another time, the face would have been handsome, almost beautiful, Dana realized, but at the moment it was stern and watchful. She was having difficulty breathing, and it suddenly felt as if the air were thin, superheated, low in oxygen. She breathed short, quick breaths too rapidly, and watched that face.

Bowie gulped, then gasped, and that triggered a gasp in Dana. They seemed to be sounds too small to be detected in the noise of the alien work area, but somehow the red Bioroid pilot became aware of the observers, whether by hearing or some higher sense.

They heard his words quite clearly, though his lips never moved. *Just as I thought: there they are!* Then he spoke directly to them, mind to mind. *Do not attempt to escape! You will remain where you are!*

Lights! Sentries: take them! the willful demigod commanded his horde. Dana, faint and panting for breath, drew on every reserve of will as she fought the red Bioroid pilot's silent compulsion. Then she felt Bowie's hand close around her upper arm, pressing her ATAC arm brassard hard into the flesh just as the fully dilated searchlights swung round beams to converge on the troopers' hiding place, and it seemed to break the spell. The blues were pounding toward them, weapons coming to bear.

Dana and Bowie slid and churned and scrambled back down the incline, abrading hands and ripping uniforms, tumbling and skidding. But in time they reached the base, already up and running. They were two ATAC regulars in superb shape; ignoring the minor hurts, hurdling boulders, they were astraddle their cycles and gunning the engines in moments.

Behind them they could already hear the racket of preparations for the chase, like the baying of hounds. And the only word of encouragement Dana had left to give her blood brother, brother in tears and in arms and in peace, was a word used carelessly by others but emphatically in the 15th squad: "Faster!"

The cycles sprang away, trailing spumes of dust in the moonlight, nearly standing on their tails, and Dana felt the naked vulnerability any tanker would in that situation. Her thought, like Bowie's, was for the safety of speed, *speed*... but there was swift pursuit on her track already, and she knew better than virtually anyone else alive how fast those Hoverplatforms moved.

The aliens had turned the gleaming, enigmatic face-plates to Zor Prime, their leader, who screamed silently, *All Bioroids to your Hovercraft!*

Then the Hoverplatforms rushed out from the landing ship, in answer to the mind command, the blues throng-ing for battle, and the red Bioroid, with the hypnotic alien inside once again, leapt high to land on its skyriding platform with sinister grace. The red came after Dana and Bowie, a very Angel of Death.

The canyon was too narrow for evasions; Dana and Bowie went high and low, rode the highside of the stone walls, and let centrifugal force pull them down, over and up again to ride the opposite wall. They crisscrossed and shot along, all the time waiting for the shot that would end their lives; alien annihilation discs crashed around them. But there was no side street; it was a flat-out race. And the swift Hoverplatforms were erasing the cycles' lead at a fearsome rate.

"Hey, Lieutenant! These androids're gonna be right on our necks in another coupla seconds!" Bowie yelled over the rush of their passage.

Androids? Now, why did I assume they're clones? Dana wondered even as she reached down for the short energy carbine strapped into its scabbard beneath her saddle. With its wirestock folded, a Hovercyclist could fire it with one hand if the need arose.

"Well, how about a little target practice, Bowie?" she called back to him, trying to sound as if she didn't have a misgiving in the world.

Bowie didn't quite achieve a smile as more discs ranged around them, detonating. "Anything's better than this!" He started freeing up his own carbine.

They got ready to turn. "Don't fire until I do."

"You got it, Dana!"

They had ridden together and trained together enough to swing their cycles in tight bootlegger turns at almost the same moment, coming end for end and charging back at the onrushing Bioroids.

"Now!" Dana leaned to one side of her handlebars, steadied her weapon with both hands, and fired. The surprise move by the cycles caught the Bioroids completely off guard. In fact, the enemy firing stopped as the aliens tried to figure out what was happening.

And some incredible luck was upon her at that moment. The carbine was a powerful small arm, but nothing compared to weapons that had already failed to down Bioroids; nevertheless, the bolt hit a startled enemy mecha and knocked it off balance, so that it fell from its Hovercraft.

Dana swerved to elude the red, and drove for the hole in the invader formation left by the toppling of the blue. For a split-second she was among the huge offworld mecha, as a crashing shook the ground, then she was beyond. Dana waited for a disc to annihilate her, but none came.

She chanced a quick look back, and realized that Bowie wasn't with her anymore. She came through another sharp turn in a shower of dust and grit, and stopped short. Far back, the red Bioroid stood with one enormous, two-toed foot crushing the smoking remains of Bowie's cycle.

And, high aloft in the vast metal fist, it held Bowie. In the strange silence following the first passage-at-arms, he lifted his head and spotted her despite the knocking-around he had been through.

More, she could hear him. "Make a run for it, Dana! Save yourself!"

This, after she had led him into this horrifying mess. "Hang on!" she hollered, and pulled her cycle's nose up and around like a rearing charger. She roared straight at the gathered Bioroids.

Bowie screamed for her to turn back, but he could see that she wasn't about to. The red felt him struggle, and closed its grip until he couldn't breathe, his ribs feeling as though they were about to give.

Dana came racing directly at the red, which waited motionlessly. Dana saw in her mind's eye the unearthly eyes of the pilot. She leaned off to one side of the saddle, firing, praying for another miracle shot.

But this time a blue jumped into place in front of the red, to shield its leader and the prisoner with its own body. Two more leapt in to flank it, and the three laid down a murderous fire with their hand weapons. Dana rode straight into it, juking and dodging, triggering madly.

All three of the aliens began to get her range, their discs converging in a coruscating nova of destruction. It was so close that it jolted her from her bike, do what she might.

Bowie, straining, saw the Hovercycle go up in a deafening thunderball. He put everything he had into one last effort to escape, to get to Dana and, if she were dead, to somehow avenge himself. But the red closed its grip tighter and he slumped, unconscious.

CHAPTER

FOURTEEN

> *Just like I tense up whenever somebody says the word "alien," there's a word that always gets Bowie sort of silent and thoughtful. Even if—and I've seen this happen—somebody innocently mentions the intermediate mode of a Veritech, Bowie sort of goes sphinx.*
>
> *And so, I react the same way, too, a bit. Nobody can say "Guardian" to me without conjuring up the image of General Rolf Emerson.*
>
> Remark attributed to Lieutenant Dana Sterling by Lieutenant Marie Crystal

WHEN BOWIE CAME TO, HE WAS STILL BEING held by the red. It was supervising from one side, as the blues picked through the wreckage of Dana's cycle. There wasn't much left, and what was was scattered wide. The Bioroids hadn't even been able to find pieces of Dana.

At a silent signal from the red, the searching stopped. There was no telling whether the humans had reported the aliens' presence; the all-important mission to recover the Protoculture Matrix took priority.

The Bioroids boarded their antigrav platforms and flew back to the mounds, where strange lights still probed sky and ground. Bowie lay helpless in the red's fist, weeping and swearing terrible vengeance.

But from a cleft of rock, a battered figure pulled itself up to watch the invaders go. Dana spat out blood, having bitten her own lip deeply and loosened some teeth in the fall. Her body felt like one big bruise. Fortunately, her tough uniform was made for this kind of thing, and had saved her from having the flesh rubbed right off her in the tumble. The many practice falls taken in training had paid off, too.

After she had been jolted from the cycle, the aliens had kept firing at it, thinking she was still aboard, unable to see it well in the midst of the explosion and raining debris. She managed to pull herself to safety outside the area where they looked for her remains.

But she could feel no gratitude. "Bowie!" She tried to draw herself up, to follow after the Bioroid pack, but whimpered in sudden agony at the pain that shot through her shoulder.

Dana was brought before General Emerson without much cleaning up and only the most cursory debriefing. Whatever she had discovered was still going on, and time was all-important. Her left arm was in a sling; the medics said it wasn't a dislocation, but it was a painful sprain. She had survived the crash better than she had any right to.

Emerson put aside the dressing-down Dana had coming for disobeying orders; there were more important matters at hand. Besides, if it hadn't been for her curiosity, Earth might very well have remained ignorant of the alien landing until it was too late—if in fact it wasn't already.

"I've been informed that you've had a closer look at these alien Bioroids," Emerson said as soon as Dana saluted and reported.

"Yes, sir. In the wasteland north of Section Sixteen."

"And a Human being, or something *like* a Human being, was operating one?"

Dana couldn't hold back a little gasp, as a sudden vision of the red Bioroid pilot came to her. "That's the way it looked from where I was hiding, sir."

Rochelle turned to his superior. "General, Human or not, what would they be looking for out in that wasteland?"

"Could they be scavengers or something, looking for salvage?" Green interjected.

Emerson shook his head irritably. Green was a steady sort as a combat leader, but the suggestion was ludicrous. These invaders had come from an advanced culture with a highly developed technology, and everything about them suggested that they had an extensive technological and social support system behind them—at least until recently.

"No, that can't be the answer." He had read the Zentraedi debriefing files as thoroughly as anyone. "They're in the service of the Robotech Masters."

Rochelle drew himself up. "Then, sir, I suggest we attack as soon as possible, before they become impossible to dislodge from their foothold."

Emerson shook his head again. "Not yet. First I want to know more about this situation, and about these Bioroids. And above all, I want to know what they're looking for."

Dana said plaintively, "But one of my men has been taken prisoner! Please, you have to let me go in there after him!"

"Permission denied." Emerson rose to his feet, no

happier with the necessities of the situation than Dana was, but in a better position to see the overall picture.

"It was your decision to return to headquarters with this intelligence. It was the correct thing to do; we're fighting for Earth's survival. A lot of lives have been lost already, and more are certain to be before this thing is over. But our mission is to repel an alien invasion, do I make myself clear?"

He did, to all those listening. They were all soldiers in a desperate war, even Bowie, who meant so much to him.

But all Dana kept hearing were those words, *it was your decision.*

At the barracks she wandered back toward the ready-room, sunk in despairing musings, until she realized someone was blocking her way.

Angelo Dante leaned against one side of the door-frame, arms folded, his foot braced against the other. "Well, well! Aren't we forgetting a little something? Where's Bowie, Lieutenant? I hear he didn't make it."

Her face went white, then flushed angrily. She tried to move past, still feeling shame and failure at Bowie's capture. "Move it, Dante."

"I call that pretty tough talk for somebody who cut and ran and abandoned that kid out there like that."

Dana made a sudden decision and met Angelo's glare. "If I *hadn't* abandoned him, there wouldn't be anybody to go out and get him back, would there?"

With her foot she swept the leg supporting all his weight from beneath him; Angelo ended up on the floor with a yelp. "Got it?" she finished with a slow smile, shucking off the sling. Her arm hurt like blazes, but this was no time to be hampered.

Angelo was looking up at her with his mouth open, not sure if he was going to jump her and give her the drubbing she had coming, or congratulate her for what she seemed to be saying.

"Sergeant, it is my considered opinion that this squad needs some night training maneuvers."

He gave her a slow smile. "Like in that off-limits area?"

She stood there and gave him a wink even while she was saying, "I don't know what you're referring to, Angie. *Ten-hut!*"

The big three-striper was on his feet with machinelike speed. "Now, then," she went on. "This squad's gotten complacent, sloppy, and out of practice. Get me?"

"Yes, ma'am!"

"Consequently, you *will* pass on the order to scramble immediately. Tell 'em to stow the yocks and grab their socks, Sergeant."

The Bioroids' activities at the mounds had come to a standstill as the Robotech Masters weighed the problems posed by the wraiths.

Progress was hampered, too, because the red Bioroid was not on the scene. He had taken the prisoner into the forward command ship to examine the Human and see what could be learned. That had proved to be vexingly little; the creature was unconscious, and its thought patterns so unevolved that normal methods of interrogation didn't work.

Bowie slowly came back to life as he felt himself being

jarred and shaken. He was still in the metallic grip of the Bioroid leader, being borne along a passageway to the sound of the massive metallic footsteps. Two blues walked behind. The place was stupendous, built to Bioroid scale.

All three mecha appeared red in the passageway's lighting. Bowie glanced around in punchy amazement; the place looked as organic as it did technological, some advanced mixture of the two. One area seemed to be composed of asymmetric spiderwebbing thicker than the thickest hawsers; the curved passageway ceiling had a vascular look, as though it were fed by blood vessels. Tremendous polished blue convexities in the wall might be darkened viewscreens or immense gemstones—Bowie couldn't even guess.

He strained at the grip, but it did no good. "C'mon, ya big ape! Lemme go! Yer crushin' me!"

The trio of Bioroids stopped before a triangular door even taller than themselves. The three door segments were joined along jagged seams, like a triskelion. As the door slid open, so did the red's broad chest and helm, exposing the glowing ball-turret and the pilot who sat there calmly, legs drawn up, looking remote and at peace.

Bowie snarled, shaking his fists. "Oh, so ya worked up the guts to show yourself, huh? Well, what happens *now*, Prince Charming? Afraid to let me go because you'd be gambling with your teeth?"

The red Bioroid pilot studied him as if he were something in a lab smear. Bowie fumed, "What's the matter, pretty boy? Can't you talk?"

The enemy spoke again in that eerie mental language.

Prisoner, you display much bravado. But like all primitives, you've yet to learn the value of silence.

And the red pilot gave Bowie a quick lesson, tossing him into the compartment that had just opened up. The Bioroid had leaned down some way, so that Bowie wasn't maimed or killed. The fall stunned him, though, knocking the wind from him.

Door and Bioroid were already resealing by the time the captive got a little breath back. "That's right! You *better* hide in that tin can, you stinking coward!"

And then the door was shut. Bowie collapsed back on the deck, hissing with the pain he hadn't let his captors see. "Just you wait, pally!"

After a while he hauled himself to his feet. The compartment he was in was as big as his whole barracks complex back at the base; surely there must be some way out.

But a hurried search yielded little. The place was evidently a storeroom, but the crates and boxes bigger than houses were impervious to his efforts to open them. He could find no escape route, not even a Bowie-size mouse hole. The enemy had neglected to take his lockback survival knife from him, but there wasn't much it could do against the armored bulkhead all around him.

Then he gave more thought to the light far overhead. It was a triangular, grilled affair, and the light source seemed to be high above the mesh. It put him in mind of conduits and crawlspaces. In another moment he was shinnying up the side of a crate, ignoring the pain of his wounds and injuries.

It took him nearly twenty minutes of scrambling, leaping, and balance-walking among the containers and pipes and structural members, and he had to double back twice to try new approaches, but at last he came up under the mesh. He hoped against hope that he wouldn't hear the rumble of the ship's engines for just a while longer—that he could get out before the invaders got whatever they had come for and departed Earth.

He hesitated, the knife in his hand. But then he went ahead, to prize up the mesh and try his best to break free. As far as he knew, he was the only one left alive to sound the alarm to all Earth that the invasion had come. Then, too, there was Dana to avenge.

The instant the knifepoint dug into the seam of the mesh where it rested against its housing, there was an intense flash of light. Bowie didn't even have time to scream; the knife flew from his hand and he dropped.

"Sir, the sun's almost up out there and a recon drone got a look at the enemy position from high altitude," Rochelle reported. "They're just beginning to excavate at the site of the old SDF-1, but we have no idea as yet what they're after or why."

Emerson stretched, yawned, and rubbed his eyes. "We can't delay any longer. Whatever they're doing, we've got to see that they don't accomplish it. They started these hostilities; now it's our turn at bat. All right, you know what I want you to do. Proceed."

Rochelle, Green, Tessel, and one or two others snapped to attention. "Yes, sir!" Then they hurried off to begin implementing the op plan Emerson had approved during the hours of consultations and meetings.

Emerson was left alone to muse. *The only thing in that old wreck is useless, rotting Robotechnology. Well, one person's junk is another's Protoculture, I suppose.*

Something about that stirred a half-developed thought in the back of his brain. There would be an avalanche of operational decisions and problems coming down on him very soon; that was a hard and fast rule with any operation. But he shunted them aside for the moment, and punched up access to the UEG archives.

CHAPTER

FIFTEEN

Dear Mom and Pop,
Things are still real quiet here, and my outfit is real rear echelon, so we're far away from the fighting, so I wish you two would stop worrying.
We've got a new commanding officer who's a woman, but she seems to be improving.
I know there's a lot of talk about the fighting right now, but don't sweat it; it's no big thing, and it'll be over soon, and then maybe I can get a furlough and come home for a while.
Say hi to everybody. I hope Pop's feeling better. The fruit-cake was great.

Love,
Your son,
Angelo Dante

Just about all the other Southern Cross units in and around Monument City had been mobilized during the night, and needed only the word to move out. The word was given.

This time, it had been decided, the TASC Veritechs, Tactical Air Force, and other flying units would stay out of it, at least for the time being. It had become obvious in the battle at Fokker Base that ground units like the ATACs were more effective against Bioroids in a surface-action situation.

Armored men and women, galvanized by the PA announcements, sprinted to their Hovertanks, troop carriers, and other vehicles. The elite MP shock troops in their powered armor suits, nonreconfigurable mecha as big as Battloids but lacking their Robotech firepower and adaptability, came marching out of their parking bays. Everywhere, the military was in motion, knowing that the enemy was now entrenched on Earth.

The Southern Cross began its deployment to draw a ring of Robotech steel around Sector Sixteen. But there were already Human defenders on the scene.

Dana peered out from under the canopy of branches that camouflaged her Hovertank. The 15th was spread through a little woodlet at the base of a rise some distance from the SDF-1's final resting place.

She again wondered about the wisdom of riding in high-gloss armor in a high-gloss mecha; certainly, the polished surfaces reflected energy shots and offered protection in that way, but as every cadet learned through backbreaking work under the watchful eyes of exacting instructors, it made them awfully hard to hide.

Now, though, she was concentrating on two blue Bioroids who were standing sentry duty on the top of the rise. One thing about the Masters' fighting mecha: they didn't seem to give a damn about concealment.

And they didn't seem to think anybody else did, either; the blues held their hand weapons and searched the sky, giving only cursory attention to the ground. Dana figured that meant that battle to them was simply straightforward charge and countercharge, in spite of the crude infantry tactics they had appeared to use in the airfield battle.

The ATACs could get only a partial glimpse of what

was going on at the excavation sight. It looked as if the labor mecha had been making test bores, and were now preparing to go at it full-choke. Dana hoped that would provide a little diversion, and cover the noise of the 15th's approach.

She counted eight blue Bioroids, spread fairly thin, guarding the part of the perimeter she planned to hit. Dana knew that a Bioroid had a lot more firepower than an ATAC, and more maneuverability if it got to its Hovercraft, but she was counting on surprise and accurate first-round fire for quick kills and a temporary advantage.

Her plan was less than subtle: a few members of the unit would make a dismounted scout and if possible get Bowie out without betraying their presence to the invaders. If that was unworkable, Dana and the 15th would burst through the perimeter, shooting up the place and inflicting all the damage they could, exploiting the edge that surprise would give them to fight their way to the forward command ship. Then the others would fight diversionary or holding actions as needed while she, Angelo, Sean, and Louie went after Bowie.

She had to admit that it wasn't the sort of thing Rommel or Robert E. Lee might have come up with, but Sean was more or less content with it. She thought Patton might have approved.

Angelo sat cracking his knuckles inside their iron gauntlets. "When d'we attack, my proud beauty?" he said softly into his helmet mike.

Like the rest, Sean sat with faceplate open so that he could breathe fresh air as long as possible, gazing up at the Bioroids through his camouflage screen. He was chewing on a piece of wild mint. "Undaunted, we advanced, to serve the principles of freedom!" he quoted in his most dramatic stage whisper. Then he spat out the mint and closed his faceplate, figuring it was just about showtime.

"'Forward through shot and shell, we went into the mouth of Hell,'" Louie added resignedly, lowering his visor, too. It fastened and sealed, and his armor was airtight. "'And pers'nally, I felt unwell, but no one there could smell, or tell—'"

"Awright, *secure* that chatter!" Dana snapped in a harsh whisper. "What d'you think is happening here, an armored assault or a Shakespeare festival?"

Angelo was about to seal up, too. "Y'know, I've got one question: what d'we do if those 'roids spot us?"

"Pray you can shoot faster and straighter than they can." Dana sealed her helmet. "Let's move out, skirmishing order—"

"Watch it, Lieutenant! Up there!" Louie yelled, but Dana had seen the blue he spotted, centered the enemy in her gunsight reticle, and fired even before Louie had finished. Even though she fired with the less-powerful nose cannon of the Hovertank mode, she shot straight and first; the blast shook the Bioroid like a toy soldier, knocking it down for keeps.

Dana was already hovering her mecha on its foot thrusters, turning it end for end and going to Gladiator mode, as she called, "Thanks, Louie! I owe you one!"

Her seat had come around so that she was facing the enemy once again, but now the long barrel of the Gladiator's main battery poked in the direction of the invaders' perimeter. The 15th knew enough about the Bioroids' silent communications by now to be sure others were on the way. "Okay, let's go!" she called.

She launched herself into the air in Gladiator mode; the rest of the 15th followed, most in Hovertank, some mechamorphosing to Gladiator in midair. Two more blues showed up to take up firing stances; Dana nailed one while she was still in the air, and Angelo got the other.

"You go look for Bowie," Angelo called. "We'll keep the bluebirds of happiness busy."

"Check." She was preparing to hop again just when another pair of blues bounded into view. Dana and Angelo leapt their Gladiators away in different directions, avoiding their first salvo. Dana blew one away while Angelo maneuvered the *Trojan Horse* around toward the other's rear flank, traversing his barrel with the speed Robotech controls allowed. The alien mecha sought to spin and take out the Gladiator behind it, but Angelo was ready, and cut it in half with one shot. Then Dana leapt *Valkyrie* again, to join him.

"You okay?" It had been a close one, like some old-time gunfight.

"Yeah," Angelo said lightly.

"We've got to get in closer!"

Hovertanks and Gladiators advanced in twenty- fifty-seventy-yard leaps now, not wanting to hurl themselves too high and so present a better target. More blues appeared to set up defensive positions; the mecha hammered and belched flame at one another. Concussions shook the ground.

"Units three, four, and five, cover the lieutenant's advance!" Angelo ordered. The ATACs went through a long-practiced advance pattern.

There was a sudden cry over the net. A blue had peppered Louie's area with raking fire, and there were smoking hotspots on the armor of the cockpit-turret of his tank, *Livewire*. Louie was screaming, arms thrown outward. Then he collapsed.

"Louie, what's wrong? You hit?" Angelo shouted over the net. The blue appeared to be surveying its handiwork, rising a bit to look down on the silent Gladiator. "Answer me, Louie!"

Louie, still unmoving, said, "Nah, I'm okay." As the blue rose up from cover a little, Louie straightened suddenly and jumped *Livewire* back, aiming the main battery as he did, greasing the enemy neatly.

"But *that* clown didn't know it!" Louie finished proudly.

"No more stunts!" Angelo barked. "Just do what I tell you!"

More Bioroids had come up to reinforce the first, taking heavy losses because the ATACs had had time to reach secure cover from which they could fire. Things were settling into a vicious, close-range firefight.

"Move in now, Lieutenant," Angelo said, "but you'd better hurry."

In another part of the alien work area, back in Hovertank mode, *Valkyrie* wended closer to the giant ship's hull using all available cover. Her visor up, Dana studied the enemy ship. It wasn't a patch on the mother ships, but was still as big as the biggest Human battlecruiser. She tried to shake off the fascination of it, tried to fight off the

fear that somehow her Zentraedi blood made her more
vulnerable to these new enemies.

Then she nearly yelled aloud. *It's him!*

It came partly as shock, partly as something she had
expected, and, deep down, even looked forward to—for
reasons she couldn't analyze—to see the red Bioroid
poised on an open deck high above. The Bioroid was
open, and its tall, slim, deep-chested pilot waited in that
characteristic pose of his, one foot on the open Robotech
breastplate, his eyes closed as if he were listening intently.

She found herself short of breath, and gave out a low
moan. *Mmmm . . .*

His eyes opened and his head came around until he
was looking straight down at her. She heard that silent,
internal voice of his again, *Hmmm . . .*

A fundamental recognition—something on profound
levels to which she had little waking access—passed between Dana and the red Bioroid pilot. This time he
shielded some of his thought from her: *This one is no
ordinary primitive! She is Of the Protoculture! She has had
open access to it; she has the power it gives!*

He watched her, unblinking, and made a sign of acknowledgment, a fey salute, hand going to brow, then
cutting away. She heard the quavery mental voice in her
head. *Know then, Primitive, that I am Zor Prime, Warlord
of the Robotech Masters!*

Dana stared at him for a moment, then lowered her
visor again. She sat looking up at him, and he stood gazing down. Neither moved.

Without warning a shot came from one side, a stray
heavy-cannon blast from a Bioroid Hovercraft. It broke
the spell; Dana maneuvered quickly, to make sure she

wasn't in anyone's line of fire. When she glanced up again, the red Bioroid was diving down like a pouncing tiger, its hand weapon held out before it.

"Try again sometime!" Dana was already springing aside, going to Gladiator mode, sending up a hail of fire. The red flipped in midair, landed nearby, and fired back. The two mecha catapulted here and there, firing and jockeying for position.

The foe got three shots into the Gladiator's side in a line, but Dana had a target of her own. She missed taking the red's right arm off, but once again got the broader target, the big discus-shaped hand weapon, knocking it away through the air.

Let's see how you do without your big metal yo-yo!

But the alien recovered like a demon, throwing a punch, rocking the Gladiator back on its thrusters and suspension.

The red behemoth was about to throw itself on the Gladiator, when Dana pulled a move she had been saving for a special, desperate moment—this moment. Her Gladiator leapt high, to come down on the red's shoulders and head with all its weight, a staggering blow that sent the crimson mecha spinning and crashing onto its back.

Dana landed well, traversed her main battery, and fired, but the red was up, vaulting high once more, with astounding speed and agility. It landed close, launching a bombshell punch near her turret, sending the Gladiator to its knees.

The alien's metal fingers sank into the Gladiator's armor as the red lifted the Gladiator in an awesome show of strength, about to tear it to pieces. Dana had no angle with the main battery, but peppered away at the lustrous visor with her rapid-fire, quad-barreled secondaries as a distraction.

She wasn't dismayed at the turn of events though; this invader still had a lot to learn about the ATACs.

Now I've gotcha! She set the Gladiators thick, immensely powerful legs against the other mecha's torso, pushing off and firing thrusters at the same time. She launched herself free, nearly toppling the red again. "I'm tired of fooling around with you!" She summoned up her mecha's Battloid form.

Her landing sent shudders through the Earth she had come to defend. "Okay, Big Red! Time to settle this!"

The red was eager; it came through the air with a tackle so fast and strong that Dana couldn't counter it. She was flipped over backward, crashing against the side of the alien ship.

Inside, the sound of the impact and its vibrations made Bowie shake his head and open his eyes. It took him a few seconds to remember where he was and figure out what had happened. The charge from the mesh hadn't killed him, and somehow he hadn't fallen all the way to the deck. He lay on a monolithic crate a few yards below where he had been standing when the power surge hit him. He checked himself for broken bones, and found none. Then the ship shook again.

"What the blazes is going on here? Hey, if you're hauling anchor, *I want off*!"

Outside, the red swung a massive punch, but its timing was off. Dana ducked, and the unbelievable power of the Bioroid (plus some power, Dana was sure, that was the red's pilot's alone) let the great scarlet fist penetrate the alien ship's hull.

Dana reacted at once, bringing her Battloid's leg up to shove the Bioroid away sprawling. As she jumped her mecha to its feet, her external pickups registered a human voice, "Well, hi, Lieutenant!"

Somehow, she wasn't surprised; although the odds of finding him, especially like this, were so remote as to be absurd. But it all fit in with the feelings that had been going through her, and the odd sensation—of hidden forces at work—that had been building in her.

"Be with you in a minute, Bowie." She turned to deal with her opponent again.

"No sweat, Dana. Lay a few on him for me!"

But the Bioroid had regained its feet as well, and now came hurtling at her like a cross between a falling asteroid and a runaway freight train. Dana rolled and scrambled, and just avoided being trampled, her Battleroid flattened. She heaved it to its feet, and decided to end the fight and get Bowie out of the ship, whatever it took.

Marquis of Queensberry rules seemed to be pretty well out the window anyway, so she didn't feel any guilt as she drew the battle rifle that had been the Hovertank's cannon moments before. The Bioroid didn't seem to know what to do. She fired from the hip, and the first shot blew the visor open.

The red flailed back and sank partway to the ground against the Masters' forward command ship. The ball turret within it was exposed amid smoking, fused components and bent armor. The shadowy form of the pilot lay inert and its pose suggested unconsciousness, or death.

The red's knees trembled, then gave, and the crimson Goliath came down like a toppled building.

Bowie was straining at the opening the red's punch had made. "It's just too narrow, Lieutenant!"

Dana brought the cannon around. "Stand away!"

With a volley of shots she widened the hole so that three troopers could have walked abreast through it. It made the air of the compartment almost too hot to endure, to breathe.

He hurried to the opening, keeping clear of its glowing, molten edges. He gathered himself, leapt through. He landed on the back of the fallen Bioroid. When he reached the ground, Bowie smiled up at Dana. "Thanks, Lieutenant."

"That's okay. It's nice and restful in the stockade; I could use a rest."

"If they need character witnesses, they'll probably make me appear for the prosecution, Dana."

CHAPTER
SIXTEEN

One might have thought the Masters, with their lesser military strength, would have perceived threats to which the mighty Zentraedi were blind.

And the Masters thought they had: they addressed the "wraiths" within the mounds, and the mecha of the Human race. How the ghosts of Khyron, Azonia, and the rest must have laughed there, deep in Tellurian soil!

Major Alice Harper Argus (ret.), *Fulcrum: Commentaries on the Second Robotech War*

BACK AT THE COMMAND CENTER, COLONEL GREEN turned to Emerson. "We just got a sitrep from the advance elements of the attack force, sir. It says that Private Bowie Grant has already been rescued."

Emerson whirled from studying the tactical displays. "Explain."

"Well, it seems that Lieutenant Sterling mobilized her squad sometime last night and performed the rescue on her own this morning. But her troops are still engaged with the enemy, and our troops are moving in to reinforce. It seems we've seen only the first round; the enemy is regrouping for another."

Emerson glanced at the maps. "And what's their strength?" He wondered if Dana would be commended or shot this time—provided she lived through the morning at all.

"Roughly equivalent to ours, from all reports, sir," Rochelle supplied. "I'd say we're pretty evenly matched."

Sean Phillips had his visor thrown back. "C'mon, Dana, get moving! What's wrong?"

"You feeling okay?" Angelo asked anxiously.

But she was not. Moments before, triumph had seemed assured. The long, slanting rays of the morning sun reminded her that only a very short time had passed since her attack commenced. Then, before she could scoop up Bowie, her external pickups brought her the creaking of armor.

"I don't believe it!" She looked down in shock. "He's coming back for *more*? It's impossible!"

But the red fist had risen again to grasp the end of her rifle-cannon's barrel, bending it, dragging it down. The weapon was useless now; she released it, backing away, placing herself between the rising Bioroid and Bowie.

"Take cover, Bowie; the rest of you watch for other Bioroids! This one's mine."

Bowie dashed away as the red reached its feet once more. It trembled but moved purposefully and unstoppably. Dana backed up cautiously, her Battloid bringing its hand up for more close combat. She had made up her mind that she was going to deck this foe for good, rip that turret out of the enemy mecha and kill or capture its occupant, or die trying. The two armored titans maneuvered like wrestlers.

Okay, whoever you are! If you can go the distance, so can I! What she couldn't see was that within his turret, the pilot's eyes were closed and he looked for all the world as if he were unconscious or dead.

Just then a fusillade of shots ranged in nearby, blowing huge chunks of soil and rock high. More came in, bracketing the two duelists. Dana looked around. "What in—"

A face appeared on one of her control console displays. Nova Satori! "Lieutenant, I have an urgent message from headquarters. The enemy's regrouping for a massive counterattack. On the other hand, your reinforcements have arrived." She allowed herself a thin smile.

There were more cannonades from the bluffs and high ground all around the advance ship. Positions where blue Bioroids had entrenched themselves or established fire superiority were pounded and roasted, pieces of enemy mecha thrown high. Dana saw Gladiators, Hovertanks, conventional armor, and even some old-style Destroids and Raider X's. There were MP-powered armor, too, much like Battloids themselves. She wondered which one Nova was in.

"Looks like the cavalry arrived just in the nick of time, eh, Dana?" Nova added.

"We'll take care of the cleanup here, Lieutenant," the Strikeforce commander's voice came up over the net. "You and your squad can back off and sit this one out. We— Huh? *What's that?*"

He was looking up because the sun had been blotted out. Something huge had come down into the morning sky. It was a ship as big as a city, floating in with an appalling, slow sureness. And there were others, all having penetrated Earth's sensor defenses, all come to punish the impudence of the primitives below. The six gargantuan mother ships of the Robotech Masters closed in from all sides. The red Bioroid stood looking up at them reverently.

The Southern Cross soldiers gripped their weapons irresolutely, barrels realigned toward the sky, but seemed feeble and ridiculous against the immense power of the starcraft.

Suddenly, the mother ships began disgorging assault craft; the bottle-shapes, several from each mother ship, flashed down at their targets. MP-powered armor, Battloid, and the rest all were caught in intense strafing, with no air cover and little ground cover. But these Earth defenders all fired back, all stood their ground and fought. Men and women hurled defiance and blazing energy salvos back into the skies—and died.

The toll was terrible, even though the attack was short; a carpet of intense radiation blasts took out many of the mecha in the surrounding heights; only Dana and her troops, close to the advance ship, were relatively safe. Conventional APCs and tanks fared even worse, sitting ducks for the assault ships. Gladiators were putting up the strongest resistance; Dana saw two of them converge their fire to bring an assault ship out of the sky in a fiery crash.

Again she heard the quavering, inhuman voice of the red. "Retreat to the forward command ship." The blues followed it away in those kangaroolike, two-legged hops, up a ramp into the ship.

They're not getting out of here because they're outgunned, that's for sure! Dana realized. She was about to yell for everyone to run for it, when an area of cloud seemed to boil away before an intense ray of light, like a beam of supernova. It sprang down into the ground near one of the mounds, though not the one containing SDF-1.

There it ignited, or exploded. A white-hot infernal wind flew out from it, riding a shockwave, carrying before it mecha, powered armor, tracked vehicles, and armored infantry. It fragmented Earth's proudest war machines, tossing them like leaves before it. In moments the formidable attack force was reduced to stunned survivors, wounded, and the many, many dead.

But the Masters had calculated well. They knew a great deal about the mounds now, knew that the Matrix would be safe for the time being—until they could return and deal with the wraiths.

Dana kept her head well down until the worst of the shockwave and heat had died away. Then she lifted her head, wiping dust from her visor, to see the forward command ship lifting away above her, moving to rejoin its mother ship. Far off to one side, a glowing crater hundreds of yards across gave testimony of the Masters' wrath.

She drew off the winged helmet tiredly, lowering it. It was a singular mercy to see Bowie wave exhaustedly from where he had taken refuge in Angelo's *Trojan Horse*.

Dana was filled with sorrow; nevertheless, she felt no guilt. Whatever the aliens wanted here, she and the others had kept it away from them.

But they'll come again. And then it'll be a fight to the death; we all know that now. A lot of good men and women died proving it today: this planet is ours! And now the Robotech Masters are going to pay!

And now she knew the name of her strangely familiar enemy: Zor.

*   *   *

In their great mother ships, the Robotech Masters pondered this latest development. The fleet of six huge ships withdrew to a geostationary orbit and remained there, silent and enigmatic.

Endless conferences took place between the Masters at their Protoculture cap and the Scientists, the Politicians, and other triumvirates at their lesser caps, and with Zor, their battlelord. The matter of the resistance of the Protoculture wraiths in the mounds was the prime source of discussion, but there were others.

For the time being there was no question of simply excavating the mound and taking the Matrix; the combined impediments of the wraiths and the Humans made that impossible. But the Masters insisted, and the Elders concurred with them, that the primitives *must* have some control over the incorporeal entities who guarded the mounds. Zor was tempted to disbelieve, but in the end agreed with their assessment when he recalled that the female he had battled was Of the Protoculture.

And yet, for reasons he could not explain to himself, he did not reveal this fact—kept all but the most perfunctory mention of Dana from his mind when reporting.

Several things became clear under the compassionless probing of the Masters: they could not take the Matrix by direct assault and dared not simply begin laying waste to the planet; their Protoculture was in short supply, and their time was running out quickly.

Because their own Protoculture sources were shrinking, the Elders grew restive, demanding some resolution.

Added to this was the fact that the Invid might become aware of the Matrix at any time, and intervene.

Using the splendid military skills and cruel, fanatic loyalty they had programmed into the last and finest of the Zor clones, Zor Prime, the Masters considered their next course of action.

A week went by.

In the UEG headquarters the military and civilian leaders of Earth's feudal government met in emergency session. They were desperate and short on sleep, and the observers who had come in from the east still had the stench of carnage and smoking ruin in their nostrils and on their clothes.

What constituted the core of the United Earth Government looked across the long table at its military hierarchy, some dozen men in a vaulted, gleaming hall. At a separate desk, facing the head of the table, sat Chairman Moran, who presided over the UEG. He was an elderly man of medium height and build, with silver-gray hair and mustache, dressed in civilian clothes adorned with the crest of the UEG. He had spent most of his life trying to reconcile the ideals of civilian freedom with the harsh necessities of military strength and preparedness.

The headquarters was a domed building of classic architecture, a new Versailles or Reichchancellory; within were fine furnishings and marble columns and rows of towering MP-powered armor to guard, but none of the men who ruled Earth took any pride or reassurance from those things today. They were disturbed and apprehensive as only the powerful, confronting an unexpected, greater power than themselves, can be.

Moran looked them over. "Gentlemen, many of you have already heard the news. This enemy military commander—Zor, or whatever his name is—has broken his self-imposed ceasefire. At oh-eight-hundred today, local time, he and his assault ships and Bioroids attacked and wiped out a training base in Sector Three. They leveled virtually every structure in that sector and killed nearly every living soul there."

The officers did know; they traded troubled glances, not knowing what to say. The attack had been so swift and merciless that there had been little time for counterattack.

"We've managed to keep word of this from getting out to the general populace, but there have been rumors," Moran went on. "And we cannot afford a panic! Now, I want to know how this could have happened. Commander Leonard, how on Earth could we be caught so completely off guard?"

Supreme Commander Leonard, top-ranking officer in Earth's military, a big bear of a man with his shaven, bullet-shaped skull and flaring brows, stood.

He rose as if he were coming at bay before a pack of hounds, glowering at Moran and the others. "Sir, I wish I could explain how they neutralize or circumvent our sensors, but I can't. Our only viable response is to strike back at once, and hard! We drove them off before and we can do it again, until they stop coming back." He shook his big fist, a gesture he often used.

Inside, he knew a bitter frustration that Zand—Zand,

who seemed to move in the shadows and had advised him so cannily before—could no longer be contacted. *Has Zand set me up?* Leonard wondered. But the man was Dr. Lang's heir on Earth, heir to the secrets of Robotech and Protoculture; elusive, furtive Zand, had sworn he was on Leonard's side. And so Leonard was determined to follow Zand's council and his own prejudices.

Moran looked to Emerson. "And what does the chief of staff have to say?"

Emerson came to his feet slowly, thinking. He didn't wish to contradict his superior, especially in that hall, but he had been called upon to speak his mind honestly. Certainly, Emerson thought that Leonard's characterization of the Masters as having been "driven away" was wide of the mark.

"Speaking candidly, sir," Emerson said, "we know next to nothing about Zor or the Robotech Masters' true capabilities. And until we do, I cannot recommend any mission that would risk our people and our ships and mecha."

Leonard, just about to sit down, slammed the table with his fist and rose up again. "Damnit, we're talking about the fate of the planet here, and about being wiped out sector by sector!"

Emerson nodded soberly. "I'm aware of that. But nothing will be gained by sacrificing our pilots to certain destruction with no hope of inflicting significant losses on the enemy."

Leonard sneered. "I won't stand for that kind of talk! You're impugning the courage and ability of our fighting forces!" Before Emerson could contradict, Leonard swung to Moran. "Those men and women have bloodied the enemy before, but good! If we let them take the offensive, they can finish the job!"

Emerson bit back his words as he heard Chairman Moran say, "Very well, Commander Leonard, prepare to attack."

Fools! thought Rolf Emerson even as he prepared to carry out the orders he was sworn to obey.

CHAPTER
SEVENTEEN

TO: Supreme Commander Leonard
FROM: Dr. Lazlo Zand, Special Protoculture Observations and Operations Kommandatura (Commanding)
  Sir:
  It is the conclusion of this unit that war against the Robotech Masters must be prosecuted as aggressively as possible, and that tactics used thus far (with particular emphasis on the Hovertank squads) still hold the best promise of positive results.

MONUMENT CITY DIDN'T FEEL MUCH LIKE A COMbat zone even though all Earth was a combat zone now, Dana reflected as she led the 15th into the middle of the downtown area on Hovercycles.

Traffic was fairly heavy and the shops, arcades, nightspots, and theaters were all brightly lit. Streetlights, traffic signals, neon signs, and even park fountains were illuminated. *Why not?* she thought. *Blackout measures are useless for hiding targets from the Robotech Masters.*

And keeping people pent up inside didn't do any good, either; there had been plenty of shelters in Sector Three, or so the scuttlebutt ran, and it hadn't helped them at all. The only thing Civil Defense restrictions would do right now was cause panic.

And panic was what the 15th was there to prevent. They were on duty, but unarmed, looking more like they were out on an evening pass. The UEG had tried to suppress rumors of the atrocities in Sector Three, but there had been the inevitable leaks. Like a lot of other Southern Cross soldiers circulating through population centers this night, the ATACs were on the lookout for any crazy inclined to jump up on a street corner soap box and proclaim Judgment Day.

Well, it sure beats a twenty-mile hike with full field pack, Sean Phillips decided, removing his goggles and readjusting his torso harness as the 15th parked their cycles side by side at the curb of a busy street. People were wandering by arm in arm, or window-shopping, taking in the sights. And there were women galore. "Well, men, this is going to be a true test of your character," he said, and got sly laughs from some of the guys.

"Ahem," said Dana, rising to face them. "All right, we start our patrols from here." She eyed them severely, then winked. "And don't do anything I wouldn't do, hmm?"

"Yes, ma'am," Sean said with a grin.

"Okay, I'll patrol the discos," somebody volunteered.

"And I'll start with that bar over there," another added with a goofy laugh.

"Yeah, you'll end with it, too," the first countered.

In another moment they were all splitting up to check out the area, all except Angelo, who gave a disgusted grunt. Duty was duty and playtime was playtime and the two shouldn't mix!

"Angie, why do I have the feeling you'd rather stay here and guard the horses?" Dana asked sweetly.

He crossed his arms and put his feet up on his handlebars. "Because you're a mind-reader, I guess."

That gave her a start, and she saw Zor's face again.

Maybe I am. But she recovered and told her troops, "Right, move out."

Which they did with a will, whopping and laughing. "Idiots," Angelo snorted.

Is every attractive female in this town grafted to some civilian's arm? Sean thought as he made his way along. Then he saw her standing by a boutique window, looking at a coat. She was small and shapely, with auburn hair to her waist and yellow slacks that did nice things for her figure.

Sean squared his uniform as he went over. *Lady, this is your lucky night!* "You seem to like that coat a lot," he said. "I admire your taste." Actually, he scarcely glanced at it.

She turned in surprise. "What?" She looked him over and broke into a dimpled smile. "Will you buy it for me, hmm?"

This was more like it. The coat *was* nice, he guessed; all scarlet embroidery and white fur trim. "Well, now, I just might be persuaded—uh!" As he read the price tag and recalled that he was now a deuce private, he went pale. *Gah! That's more than I make in a year!*

"On second thought, red's not your color," he improvised. "Listen, why don't you and me go someplace and get ourselves a drink, yes?" He winked.

She made a wry face and removed the hand he'd settled lightly on her shoulder. "Thanks anyway. Maybe some other time." She said it walking.

"Sure, anytime you say!" he called after. *Maybe I sounded too insincere? Well, it's her loss.*

* * *

Two blocks away, Dana was looking into another boutique window, considering a nice little evening frock that looked just about right for her. A hand fell on her shoulder and she pivoted, ready to show some masher what Hovertank officers learned in hand-to-hand.

But she was facing a smug-looking Angelo Dante. "Time to spit on the fire and call in the hounds," he said. "We just got a general recall to base. Something big is up."

The 15th was back on standby alert, manning their Hovertanks and waiting. This show was reserved for the TASCs and the Cosmic Units.

Fokker Base had been rebuilt hastily. Barely twenty-four hours after the raid on Sector Three, the light of morning showed a half-dozen shuttles at the vertical and ready to launch. Final preparations were under way, and people were running for bunkers and observation posts.

The shuttles launched, the first battle wing of the planned strike. On the other side of the base, the Black Lions and the other Veritech outfits waited, the second battle wing. When the shuttles were away and clear, the VTs got the green light. With Maria Crystal leading, the fighters thundered down the runway to even the score with the Robotech Masters.

Leonard came into the command center to find Emerson bent over the illuminated displays. Leonard had regained his composure, especially in light of the fact that Emerson was his most capable subordinate. To put it more truthfully, over the years Leonard had garnered credit for many things that had been Emerson's accomplishments.

Leonard dropped a thick hand on the flared shoulderboard of Emerson's torso harness. "Believe me, Rolf, this is the only way."

Emerson studied him for a long time before replying, "I hope to God you're right."

The VTs went in first, loosing swarms of missiles at the enemy flagship, their sole objective. But the missiles were no sooner away than globes of light boiled out of the flagship, like enormous will-o'-the-wisps, bursting into hexagonal webs of pulsating light like gigantic snowflakes.

The snowflakes moved and drifted into position, intersecting the missiles' paths, and the Earthly ordnance detonated harmlessly against them. The other mother ships were silent and dark but for running lights, waiting.

Still more of the energy snowflakes came forth, until a net of them protected the flagship. The VTs swept around for another try, and this time beams from the chandelier-bulb cannon crackled across empty space. More than forty fighters were lost in the first ninety seconds of the massed attack on the flagship. Still the VTs swung around for another go, hoping against hope to get in under the hexagons and deliver a blow.

But they were flying straight into a murder machine.

"Attack groups two and eight have disengaged from the enemy," the flat, synthesized voice of the intel computer echoed in the command center. "Groups three, four, and seven report heavy losses. Other groups fail to respond to transmissions and are believed to have been totally destroyed."

Leonard turned to Emerson angrily but also, people in the command center could see, with a tremble of fear. "How can this be happening to us?"

Emerson chose to ignore him, except to observe, "So far we haven't even put a dent in them." He looked to Rochelle. "Any sign of a counterattack yet?"

"Negative at this time, sir. They're standing pat."

Emerson called for an update on losses. The computer printed out the awful facts and figures. Three quarters of the attack wings' forces were gone, immolated in a few minutes.

"All those men and women lost," Emerson murmured, scanning the list.

"It's—it's a disaster," Leonard said unsteadily. He turned and lurched toward the door.

Emerson didn't even bother to solicit Leonard's permission. "Call off the attack! All units disengage and return to base." Then he turned and glared at Leonard's back as the supreme commander exited.

Not far away, there was a different kind of battle being fought in the UEG's foremost Robotech research laboratory, in the military-industrial facility near the airbase. And this battle was turning, slowly, in the Human race's favor.

Dr. Miles Cochran and his colleague, Dr. Samson Beckett, were two of the hottest of the Robotech hotshots who had trained under Dr. Emil Lang and, later, Dr. Lazlo Zand. Now they pored over the remains of a downed blue Bioroid that lay on a worktable like the world's biggest cadaver awaiting the championship autopsy of all time.

Its guts were opened up and wired to every monitoring device the lab had. It looked like it was sprouting a garden of sensor wires, photo-optic lines, monitoring circuits, and computer links.

Cochran, a thin-faced, intense redhead, said, "I'm activating ultraviolet scanner, Sam."

Beckett, smaller and dark-haired, wearing tinted glasses, was *ooh*ing and *aah*ing over the things he was encountering with his probes, but stopped to step back and watch.

The scanner came down to irradiate the Bioroid's entire form, passing from crown to toes, coordinating with readouts and analysis computers, scrutinizing every part of the shattered mecha.

The two went to the computer screens to see what they came up with. The data banks were linked in with recordings and sketches of the mecha the Southern Cross forces had fought thus far. The two watched the information and diagrams flash, the light reflecting off Beckett's glasses.

"What about the damage received?" Cochran asked. "See if you can get me a readout on that." Beckett bent to the task.

He got an integrated analysis of the internal structure of the mecha. There was severe mechanical damage because a leg had been ripped off in battle, but no physical explanation as to why all systems were so completely inert despite the Humans' efforts to activate them. Then they got the confirmation they were looking for.

"Definite traces of biogenetic material," Beckett said flatly.

"So there *was* something alive in there, something that escaped before the mop-up crew got to the scene, or self-destructed. Can you give us a look-see at what it was?"

"I can try." Beckett bent to his task again. The most powerful medical and genetic engineering programs were accessed, a stupendous amount of computer power. Alongside a detailed DNA blueprint, the computer drew up a human form. "Unbelievable," Beckett breathed.

"It's Human! Not simply *like* us, as the Zentraedi were, but *Human*!"

"But—it's from outside the Solar System!" Beckett was shaking his head. "Maybe . . . somehow they're from Hunter's SDF-3 expedition?"

It was Cochran's turn to shake his head. "No. But those ATAC tankers were right; they saw what they thought they saw."

Beckett removed his glasses. "God! Wait till Zand hears this! He'll freak!"

There was a chuckle from the darkness; Cochran and Beckett spun toward it even as they realized they knew who it was. "Perhaps that is too extreme a word, Samson. Let's just say that I'm —*pleased*."

Dr. Lazlo Zand came a little farther into the light, so that his eerie eyes could be seen. "And of course my little Dana was right! Of course your findings bear me out! The Protoculture weaves, it spins, it manipulates and *shapes*, young doctors! Its ability to shape mere machinery is nothing next to its ability to shape *events*!"

He stepped a little closer still, studying the Bioroid. He was a man of medium height, in unornamented UEG attire, his hair still unruly after all these years. His eyes seemed to be all iris, as Lang's had been ever since Lang had taken that Protoculture boost aboard the SDF-1 when it first landed. Only, in Zand's case, the transformation hadn't taken place until years later. He looked no less unearthly than a Robotech Master.

"You've done well, but now you must double-check your findings to be sure there is no error in your presentation when you take them to the UEG."

Cochran found his voice. How had Zand gotten into the lab? How had he known what Beckett and Cochran were doing there? They hadn't seen or had word of or about him in years. Yet, those weren't questions Cochran felt safe in asking, so he said, "Surely, Dr. Zand, you'll want to accompany us and elaborate on—"

"No!" Zand raised a warning finger. "No mention of me, understood? Good! Now, back to work, both of you." Zand turned for the door.

"But when will you—" Beckett began.

"When the time is right," Zand said, silhouetted against the light from outside, "you will hear from me again."

Emerson rested his chin on his interlaced fingers. "And so you're saying Zor is a Human being, and not a miniaturized Zentraedi?"

Beckett and Cochran nodded.

"Then Dana and Bowie were right," Emerson said softly, staring into space. "And we're fighting our own kind. Like brothers slaughtering each other."

Just then Rochelle buzzed Emerson with the final compilation of the battle casualties. Eighty-five VTs destroyed, seven damaged beyond repair; five shuttles destroyed, one damaged beyond repair. Two-hundred-seven pilots and aircraft crew people dead, another twenty ground support and two-hundred-odd civilians dead, the latter two figures from crashes of damaged aircraft. Eighty-seven missing in action and unaccounted for, presumed to be adrift in space, dead or alive.

In the ready-room at the 15th, for once the banter was all but nonexistent.

"Worst defeat of the war," Bowie said, stretching out the kinks that wearing armor always gave him, grateful to be back in a simple uniform.

"And that was only one ship," Sean reminded him.

"I tell ya, the VTs coulda got through if they hadn't've been called off," Angelo insisted. "Look what we did to those ali—those XTs on the Liberty mission."

Dana made no response to the fact that he hadn't used the word *aliens*, but she noticed that nobody in the 15th used it when referring to the enemy now. It moved her so, their literally unspoken support of her—she very warily felt them to be the family she'd never had.

Louie looked up from the calculations he was doing on a lap-size computer. "And I'm telling *you*, Angie, that that ship's design makes a frontal assault a complete impossibility."

Sean chortled. "I forgot: the professor, there, knows everything!"

Louie held his temper, used to this kind of flak. Bright and inventive enough for any tech school or advanced degree program, he had still opted for the ATACs. He liked being a corporal in a line outfit and, more to the point, the tinkering and computer hacking and equipment modifications he did were done without some frowning lab-coat type looking over his shoulder. He was also confident that the studying and research he did on his own, open-ended, put him way ahead of the people who had to complete course requirements in any school.

Dana put in, "But Zor's ship must have *some* weak spot."

Louie turned the dark-goggled gaze on her, nodding. "Exactly right. To start with, I figure that Zor's ship is not powered by an engine as we would recognize one."

"Huh?" Dana said. "Then how's it get around?"

"Well, it can travel between the stars by spacefolding, of course, like the SDFs and the Zentraedi," Louie explained. "And to get around over smaller distances, it has a more localized folding process, a sort of a twisting of opposing forces, like squirting a grape seed between your fingers."

Dana remembered some of the theory and jargon Louie had spouted in sessions past. "So, if you upset the hyper-balance, you've got yourself an unstable ship."

Sean caught her thoughtful tone and looked her over. "What exactly are you thinking about?"

She gave him a closed-face look. "Basic military strategy." She rose, took a few paces, then turned back to them. "C'mon, Louie, we've got work to do!"

CHAPTER
EIGHTEEN

Lazlo, my valued colleague,
*   It falls upon me to leave now with the SDF-3 expedition,*
and falls to you to stay, for reasons we both know.
*   But I ask you to keep in mind the fact that my Awakening*
to the Protoculture was in some measure accidental, while
yours was fully aforethought, and that certain intents and pur-
poses in you are at times very strong.
*   I exhort you to remember that you will be dealing with*
HUMAN BEINGS, and to work contrary to their wellbeing
will be in some measure, always, to work at cross purposes
with the Protoculture. Please don't let the eagerness to plumb
the depths of Protoculture distort your thinking.

Your friend,
Emil Lang

WHEN DANA APPEARED AT THE ROBOTECH RE-
search lab with Louie in tow, she had the impression that
Drs. Cochran and Beckett were looking at her rather
strangely, at least at first.

But she shrugged it off; research types were always off
somewhere in a world of their own. Besides, Louie had
them totally fascinated with his idea in short order. First
thing she knew, Louie was sitting at Beckett's main computer terminal with the doctors looking on, bringing up
diagrams and displays and equations and computer-
generated images to explain and verify his analysis.

"It's only a theory, I admit," he said as the computer

illuminated various parts of a grid-diagram of Zor's vessel. "But after all, no scans show any central power source, am I right?"

Cochran nodded, lower lip between his thumb and forefinger, staring into the screen. Louie went on. "But I, um, I accessed the intel computers and I found what's gotta be a bio-gravitic induction network."

The computer showed it, a convoluted array like a highway system or blood vessels, picked out in neon red. "There seems to be some kind of perpetual bio-gravitic cycle; the Protoculture quanta are simultaneously attracted to and repelled by one another. Kinda like what's going on in the sun, if you want to put it that way, gravity and fusion fighting it out in a sort of equilibrium."

Dana tried to get a word in edgewise, but the three men were completely caught up in their tech-talk.

Beckett did sneak in a sidelong look at her, though. How had Dana, of all people, come to be the one to find this Louie Nichols, this gem-in-the-rough genius/weirdo? Of course it was again in total defiance of any coincidence, and Beckett had renewed awe for Protoculture's power to shape events.

"It appears to effect these two strong mega-forces," Louie said.

"Through phased bonding!" Cochran comprehended, grinning from ear to ear.

Dana was tired of hearing about the framistat field connected to the veeblefertzer anomalies. "So if we destabilize this equilibrium of yours, we'll knock the whole ship out of whack, right?"

They frowned at her coarse language, but Louie shrugged. "Yes. At least theoretically."

She looked to Cochran and Beckett. "Then you find the right spot and we'll see that the job gets done!"

Cochran hedged. "I don't think the chief of staff will choose you for the mission, Lieutenant. Not with your track record."

But inside he was wondering how Zand could let the girl run around loose like this, constantly daring aliens to shoot her cute blond head off. She was the very core of so much of Zand's work and planning.

Ah, but that's the heart of the matter, isn't it? he seemed to hear Zand lecturing. It's Protoculture that shapes events, and living beings interfered with it or sought to hamper it only at their own peril.

Zand, and even the great Lang, had realized this very early on; only by being observers of events and learning the innermost secrets of Protoculture—the ones that had died with the original Zor—could they ever hope to reach a point where they dared try to *manipulate* its greatest powers.

Dana was saying cheerfully, "Oh, I beg to differ. The Fifteenth is the perfect choice for this mission!"

Getting Bowie to agree to help her talk Emerson into letting the 15th take the mission was only slightly more difficult than getting a mule into high heels. But he saw that the rest of the 15th was all for it, so he gave in at last.

In Emerson's office, Dana, Bowie, and Louie held their collective breath while Emerson studied the data. "Sir, we've finally got the weapon we need to hit the Robotech Masters where it hurts," Bowie prompted.

Emerson brought his chair back around. "It's an in-

sane mission. Hopeless. And we can't spare the pilots or
VTs."

Dana gave him her best wide-eyed look. "But who said
anything about Veritechs? Looks more like a job for
Hovertanks, I was thinking, General."

Emerson moaned inwardly and wished for the days
when he could paddle them when they had been bad and
send them to bed without supper. And there had been
quite a few those.

But that was before the days when they were soldiers
who had sworn an oath of duty. And before the days
when the Robotech Masters had come to grind the Earth
to rubble beneath an iron heel. "You think you can do
it?"

Her gaze was level now, her nod slow and sure. "Yes,
sir."

Emerson rose. "Good hunting, people."

Again the fighters went up, but this time they were as
cautious as they could manage to be, firing from a distance, putting more emphasis on evasive maneuvers than
on accuracy. Once more the glowing, throbbing hexagonal webs appeared. Dana thought how much like power-
veined snowflakes they looked.

The snowflakes moved, as they had before, to supply
coverage to heavily attacked areas, leaving others more
lightly guarded. It was something intel had noted on the
first assault; the time had come to use it.

The shuttle pilot flying the mission was a chill cube;
when a stray Masters cannon round grazed the fuselage of
his ship, he said offhandedly, "Just a flesh wound, pards.
Goin' in."

He stood the ship on its side to make it between two of the spiral ziggurat megastructures on the deck below, then flew along a trench, well aware that a speed slow enough to make a combat drop was too slow to dodge enemy flak. He shrugged and kept flying. "Made it through," he thought to mention to the ATACs back in the drop bay, as if telling them that the mail had arrived.

"Outta the frying pan," Dana heard Sean mutter into his helmet mike. Then the pilot gave the order to open the drop bay door, and they were looking out at the onrushing techno-terrain of the mother ship's upper hull.

The Hovertanks' engines were already revving. The ATACs roared out in order, dropping into deployment pattern as they descended to the hull.

"Everyone accounted for?" Dana, in the lead, asked. She was trying to take in everything at once, looking for AA emplacements and other wicked surprises, spot her target, see how the battle was going, and make sure *Valkyrie* was functioning right.

Angelo, farther back, reported, "Roger that; everybody's in position, Lieutenant."

The ATACs barreled along, lining up on their leader according to assignment. "All right, boys; you know the drill."

They did; it was Sterling-simple. They were to follow Dana's targeting program, pierce the hull, and expose that bio-gravitic network. Then they would concentrate fire, disrupt the energy highway system, and put the mother ship's lights out.

Unless any of ten thousand things went wrong. Bowie sang out a Southern Cross Army refrain, "Just another day in the SCA!"

They stayed in a long trench for cover, and had good luck for an astoundingly tranquil ten seconds before trouble reared its armored head. "Uh-oh, we got company," Sean noted. Four Bioroids had dropped down into the trench, far ahead, to block their way. Dana found herself holding her breath, wondering what color they were.

Well, if Big Red's in my way now, it's his tough luck! She made an obscene reference to what the Bioroids could go and do. "Forget 'em! It's that system we're after! Close up behind me!"

They did, and Dana hit emergency thrust. She dodged the enemy mecha's shots and was upon them before they got their bearings, bowling them over with the solid weight of her tank, not bothering to shoot. All were blues. The 15th howled like werewolves and followed her on toward the target.

"The shuttle got in under their defensive shields," Rochelle told Emerson. "We register a running firefight on the upper hull, sir."

Emerson inclined his head in acknowledgment but didn't take his eyes from the displays.

Bioroids closed in from both sides and behind, but none were on their Hovercraft, and so it remained a road-race. Trooper Thornton heard Sean's warning but couldn't dodge in time, and a wash of annihilation discs blew out the folded Bioroid hand in its nacelle under his tank's left rear armor skirt.

"Been hit, Lieutenant," Thornton drawled, trying for damage control. But the decrease in speed let two Bioroids catch up to him; they dropped feetfirst onto his ship, disintegrating it in a fireball, and kept on coming.

"Louie! Battloid mode!" Dana called.

The Bioroids were fighting on their home ground, but the ATACs had the advantage of velocity, adrenaline, and a desperate need to carry out their mission. Dana and Louie mechamorphosed in mid-turn, and went rocketing back at the enemy as ultratech knights, weapons blazing. This time they used the main battery, the heavy Gladiator cannon that was usually stored in the Battloid's right arm but could be brought forth in extreme need. Everything around them seemed to be happening in slow motion.

They got the first Bioroid as it was still charging, the second and third when the enemy mecha stopped to shoot it out, and the fourth when it sought to withdraw and had its route blocked by a dikelike structural feature.

"Better luck next time," Dana bade the last to go, but as it went it toppled into a sort of utility groove. Its explosion set off another, greater one, and the groove became a crackling, Protoculture-hot version of an old-time blackpowder fuse.

Dana gasped as the eruption raced along the groove, sending up a curtain of starflame behind it, blowing armored deckplates high, moving as fast as any Hovertank. The racing superfuse reached a low, pillbox feature on the hull and went up like a roman candle.

"Louie, did we do it?"

Louie's helmet gave him buglike look, but beneath it he was smiling wide.

"Yes, ma'am! We've found the bio-gravitic network!"

"Let's get it!" She raced in with a dozen and more Battloids covering and bringing up the rear, moving like veteran infantry, or SWAT cops. They fired with all the staggering power the Hovertanks could bring to bear; Bioroids, unused to such house-to-house, room-to-room type—combat, were at the disadvantage, and took all the losses then.

One Bioroid almost blasted Dana, but she stumbled out of its way and Angelo got the Bioroid instead, shooting it off a tall tower so that it fell a long way to the hull, somersaulting, like something out of an old western.

Dana came up with her Battloid's head hanging over the brink of a shaft exposed by the exploded pillbox. The shaft was so deep that she couldn't see the bottom.

"You found it, ma'am," Louie observed. "Down there's the processing field that manages the energy equilibrium. If we blow up the equipment down at the field intersection locus, we'll destabilize this whole damn garbage scow."

Dana had regained her feet. "Let's do-it-to-it!" She studied the diagram Louie was sending her, and armed the heavy missile she was carrying for the purpose. All of them had one—just one apiece—but Dana wanted this shot to be hers.

Nearby, the 15th was in a furious firefight with the Bioroids as more and more enemy reinforcements showed up. The weapons beams spat and veered, seeking targets; the annihilation discs flew.

Sean yelled, "Dana, we've got ya covered, but there're more 'roids crashing the party!"

"Hang on!" She adjusted the range on the missile, and its dial-a-yield for maximum explosive force. Alien discs began ranging in around her, and Louie turned the *Live-*

wire to give more covering fire. "Lieutenant, I really suggest you hurry!"

"Jump, all you guys! Go! Don't wait for me!" She released the missile and watched its corkscrew trail disappear down into the blackness. Then she turned to propel herself into space with the strength of her Battloid's legs and the thrusters built into its feet, breaking out of the surface gravity field around the upper hull. She saw that the other Battloids were already in the air. As she went, her instruments registered a direct hit.

The Bioroids were trying to shoot down the ascending Battloids when the column of white light and raw destruction shot from the shaft, like Satan's own artillery spewing forth. The Battloids were already up and speeding away from it, but the Bioroids closing in on the shaft to see what damage had been done got a final, horrific surprise.

The gush of unleashed energy set off explosions in and around the shaft; a dozen blues were whirled away like leaves in a hurricane, molten metal, dismembered by the force of the blast, twisted into unrecognizable shapes as the volcano of energy blew higher and higher.

"Looks like you knew what you were talking about, Louie," Sean said in a subdued voice, thinking what they were all thinking: the explosion surpassed all estimates and projections; if they had hung around for another few seconds, the 15th would have been history, too.

Then everybody was making ribald praise of the Cosmic Units as the shuttle came into view, right on pickup vector. Dana looked at the lapsed-time function on her mission displays and realized in shock that the whole thing had taken only a few minutes.

"We see you, transport; get ready to take us aboard."
Her elation was complete, for now.

Dana and the rest of the 15th, the Cosmic crews, and
the TASC fliers could all see the secondary explosions
ripping along the mother ship's hide as the ATACs dove
aboard the shuttle. Furious fires burned out of control,
becoming thermonuclear bonfires in the escaping atmosphere; the monster ship swung to in accordance with
whatever motive forces it employed; its orbit decayed at
once.

Dana watched over an optical pickup patched through
from the shuttle bridge. She felt vast satisfaction, a quell-
ing of her own fear and self-doubt.

Then the satisfaction retreated; the moment she
touched down she would have to begin getting and training replacement personnel and mecha. It was plain the
15th would be needed again very soon.

Because the mother ship was beginning a long, controlled fall toward Earth.

"It's breaking up!" Emerson exclaimed, watching the
relayed image.

"Only peripherally, sir," Tessel noted, reading another
display.

"I never would've believed it," Rochelle commented
quietly. He turned and called out a command, "Ready-
reaction force, stand by for immediate deployment!"

"Once you have Zor's landing point plotted, seal it off
and ring it in with defense in depth," Emerson instructed
quietly. "Air, ground, subterranean listening equipment
—everything!"

"Yes, sir!"

Emerson watched the listing mother ship, a wounded dinosaur helpless to stop its plunge. Bigger than a city, it settled toward a final resting spot in the hills above Monument City. Emerson wondered if that was by calculation. He was beginning to abandon all faith in coincidence.

The controlled crash didn't destroy the mother ship, nor did Emerson expect it to; that would have been too much to hope for. It loomed like a colossal glacier of metal, silent and challenging.

Very well, he thought. *Challenge accepted.*

He turned to Rochelle. "Oh, and Colonel."

"Sir?"

"Tell the Fifteenth to stand down for a little rest; they've earned it."

The following chapter is a sneak preview of *Metal Fire*— Book VIII in the continuing saga of ROBOTECH!!

CHAPTER
ONE

EXEDORE: *So, Admiral, there is little doubt: [Zentraedi and Human] genetic makeup points directly at a common point of origin.*
ADMIRAL GLOVAL: *Incredible.*
EXEDORE: *Isn't it. Furthermore, while examining the data we noticed many common traits, including a penchant on the part of both races to indulge in warfare. . . . Yes, both races seem to enjoy making war.*

From Exedore's intel reports to the SDF-2 High Command

ONCE BEFORE, AN ALIEN FORTRESS HAD CRASHED on Earth . . .

Its arrival had put an end to almost ten years of global civil war; and its resurrection had ushered in armageddon. That fortress's blackened irradiated remains lay buried under a mountain of earth, heaped upon it by the very men and women who had rebuilt the ship on what would have been its island grave. But unbeknownst to those who mourned its loss, the soul of that great ship had survived the body and inhabited it still—an entity living in the shadows of the technology it animated, waiting to be freed by its natural keepers, and until then haunting the world chosen for its sorry exile. . . .

This new fortress, this most recent gift from heaven's more sinister side, had announced its arrival not with tidal and tectonic upheavals but with open warfare and devastation—death's bloodstained calling cards. Nor was this fortress derelict and uncontrolled in its fateful fall but driven, brought down to Earth by the unwilling minor players in its dark drama. . . .

"ATAC Fifteen to air group!" Dana Sterling yelled into her mike over the din of battle. "Hit 'em again with everything you have! Try to keep their heads down! They're throwing everything but old shoes at us down here!"

Less than twenty-four hours ago her team, the 15th squad Alpha Tactical Armored Corps, had felled this giant, not with sling and shot, but with a coordinated strike launched at the fortress's Achilles' heel—the core reactor governing the ship's bio-gravitic network. It had dropped parabolically from geosynchronous orbit, crash-landing in the rugged hills several miles distant from Monument City.

Hardly a *coincidental* impact point, Dana said to herself as she bracketed the fortress on the sights of the Hovertank's rifle/cannon.

The 15th, in Battloid mode, was moving across a battle zone that was like some geyser field of orange explosions and high-flung dirt and rock—a little like a cross between a moonscape and the inside of Vesuvius on a busy day.

Up above, the TASC fighters, the Black Lions among them, roared in for another pass. The glassy green tear-drop-cannon of the fortress didn't seem as effective in atmosphere, and so far there had been no sign of the snowflake-shields. But the enemy's hull, rearing above the assaulting Battloids, still seemed able to soak up all the punishment they could deal it and stand unaltered.

An elongated hexagon, angular and relatively flat, the alien fortress measured over five miles in length, half that in width. Its thickly plated hull was the same lackluster gray of the Zentraedi ships used in the First Robotech War; but in contrast to those organic leviathan dreadnaughts, the fortress boasted a topography to rival that of a cityscape. Along the long axis of its dorsal surface was a mile-long raised portion of superstructure that resembled the peaked roofs of many twentieth-century houses. Forward was a concentrically coiled conelike projection Louie Nichols had christened "a Robotech teat"; aft were massive Reflex thruster ports; and elsewhere, weapons stations, deep crevices, huge louvered panels, ziggurats, onion domes, towers like two-tined forks, stairways and bridges, armored docking bays, and the articulated muzzles of the ship's countless segmented "insect leg" cannons.

Below the sawtooth ridge the pilots of the fortress had chosen as their crash site was Monument City, and several miles distant across two slightly higher ridges, the remains of New Macross and the three Human-made mounds that marked the final resting place of the super dimensional fortresses.

Dana wondered if the SDF-1 had something to do with this latest warfare. If these invaders were indeed the Robotech Masters (and not some other band of XT galactic marauders), had they come to avenge the Zentraedi in some way? Or worse still—as many were asking—was Earth fighting a new war with micronized Zentraedi?

Child of a Human father and a Zentraedi mother—the only known child of such a marriage—Dana had good reason to disprove this latter hypothesis.

That *some* of the invaders were Humanoid was a fact only recently accepted by the High Command. Scarcely a month ago, Dana had been face-to-face with a pilot of one of the invaders' bipedal mecha—the so-called Bioroids. Bowie Grant had been even closer, but Dana was the one who had yet to get over the encounter. All at once the war had personalized itself; it was no longer machine against machine, Hovertank against Bioroid.

Not that that mattered in the least to the hardened leaders of the UEG. Since the end of the First Robotech War, Human civilization had been on a downhill slide; and if it hadn't come to Humans facing aliens it probably would have been Humans against Humans.

Dana heard a sonic roar through the Hovertank's external pickups and looked up into a skyful of new generation Alpha fighters, snub-nosed descendants of the Veritechs.

The place was dense with smoke and flying fragments from missile bursts, and the missiles' twisting tracks. As Dana watched, one pair of VTs finished a pass only to have two alien assault ships lift into the air and go up after them. Dana yelled a warning over the Forward Air Control net, then switched from the FAC frequency to her own tactical net because the real showdown had begun: two blue Bioroids had popped up from behind boulders near the fortress.

The blues opened fire and the ATACs returned it with interest; the range was medium-long, but energy bolts and annihilation discs skewed and splashed furiously, searching for targets. At Dana's request, a Tactical Air Force fighter-bomber flight came in to drop a few dozen tons of conventional ordnance while the TASCs got set up for their next run.

Abruptly, a green-blue light shone from the fortress,

and a half second later it lay under a hemisphere of spin-driftlike stuff, a dome of radiant cobweb, and all incoming beams and solids were splashing harmlessly from it.

But the enemy could fire through their own shield, and did, knocking down two of the retreating bombers and two approaching VTs with cannonfire. Whatever the damage to the bio-gravitic system was, it plainly hadn't robbed the fortress of all its stupendous power.

Dana's hand went out for the mode selector lever. She attuned her thoughts to the mecha and threw the lever to G, reconfiguring from Battloid to Gladiator. The Hovertank was now a squat, two-legged Self-Propelled Gun, with a single cannon stretching out in front of it.

Nearby, in the scant cover provided by hillside granite outcroppings and dislodged boulders, the rest of the 15th —Louie Nichols, Bowie Grant, Sean Phillips, and Sergeant Angelo Dante among others—similarly reconfigured, unleashing salvos against the stationary fortress.

"Man, these guys are tough as nails!" Dana heard Sean say over the net. "They aren't budging an inch!"

And they aren't likely to, Dana knew. *We're fighting for our home, they're fighting for their ship and their only hope of survival.*

"At this rate the fighting could go on forever," Angelo said. "Somebody better think of something quick." And everyone knew he wasn't talking about sergeants, lieutenants, or anybody else who might be accused of working for a living; the brass better realize it was making a mistake, or come evening they would need at least one new Hovertank squad.

Then Angelo picked up on a blue that had charged

from behind a rock and was headed straight for Bowie's *Diddy-Wa-Diddy*. The attitude and posture of Bowie's mecha suggested that it was distracted, unfocused.

Damn kid, woolgathering! "Look out, Bowie!"

But then Sean appeared in Battloid mode, firing with the rifle/cannon, the blue stumbling as it broke up in the blazing beams, then going down.

"Wake up and stay on your toes, Bowie," Angelo growled. "That's the third time today ya fouled up."

"Sorry," Bowie returned. "Thanks, Sarge."

Dana was helping Louie Nichols and another trooper try to drive back blues who were crawling forward from cover to cover on their bellies, the first time the Bioroids had ever been seen to do such a thing.

"These guys just won't take no for an answer," Dana grated, raking her fire back and forth at them.

Remote cameras positioned along the battle perimeter brought the action home to headquarters. An intermittent beeping sound (like nonsense Morse) and horizontal noise bars disrupted the video transmission; still the picture was clear: the Tactical Armored units were taking a beating.

Colonel Rochelle vented his frustration in a slow exhale of smoke, and stubbed out his cigarette in the already crowded ashtray. There were three other staff officers with him at the long table, at the head of which sat Major General Rolf Emerson.

"The enemy is showing no sign of surrender," Rochelle said after a moment. "And the Fifteenth is tiring fast."

"Hit them harder," Colonel Rudolph suggested.

"We've got the air wing commander standing by. A surgical strike—nuclear, if we have to."

Rochelle wondered how the man had ever reached his current rank. "I won't even address that suggestion. We have no clear-cut understanding of that ship's energy shield. And what if the cards don't fall our way? Earth would be finished."

Rudolph blinked nervously behind his thick glasses. "I don't see that the threat would be any greater than the attacks already launched against Monument."

Butler, the staff officer seated opposite Rudolph, spoke to that. "This isn't 'War of the Worlds,' Colonel—at least not yet. We don't even know what they want from us."

"Do I have to remind you gentlemen about the attack on Macross Island?" Rudolph's voice took on a harder edge. "Twenty years ago isn't exactly ancient history, is it? If we're going to wait for an *explanation*, we might as well surrender right now."

Rochelle was nodding his head and lighting up another cigarette. "I'm against escalation at this point," he said, smoke and breath drawn in.

Rolf Emerson, gloved hands folded in front of him on the table, sat silently, taking in his staff's assessments and opinions but saying very little. If it were left up to him to decide, he would attempt to open up a dialogue with the unseen invaders. True, the aliens had struck the first blow, but it had been the Earth forces who had been goading them into continued strikes ever since. Unfortunately, though, he was not the one chosen to decide things; he had to count on Commander Leonard for that. . . . *And may Heaven help us*, he thought.

"We just can't let them *sit* there!" Rudolph was insisting.

Emerson cleared his voice, loud enough to cut through the separate conversations that were in progress, and the table fell silent. The audio monitors brought the noise of battle to them once again; in concert, permaplas windowpanes rattled to the sounds of distant explosions.

"This battle requires more than just hardware and manpower, gentlemen. . . . We'll give them back the ground we've taken because it's of no use to us right now. We'll withdraw our forces temporarily, until we have a workable plan."

The 15th acknowledged the orders to pull back and ceased fire. Other units were reporting heavy casualties, but their team had been fortunate: seven dead, three wounded—counts that would have been judged insignificant twenty years ago, when Earth's population was more than just a handful of hardened survivors.

Emerson dismissed his staff, returned to his office, and requested to meet with the supreme commander. But Leonard surprised him by telling him to stay put, and five minutes later burst through the door like an angry bull.

"There's got to be some way to crack open that ship!" Leonard railed. "I will not accept defeat! I will not accept the status quo!"

Emerson wondered if Leonard would have accepted the status quo if he had sweated out the morning in the seat of a Hovertank, or a Veritech.

The supreme commander was every bit Emerson's opposite in appearance as well as temperament. He was a massive man, tall, thick-necked and barrel-chested, with a huge, hairless head, and heavy jowls that concealed what had once been strong, angular features, Prussian features, perhaps. His standard uniform consisted of white britches, black leather boots, and a brown longcoat fringed at the shoulders. But central to this ensemble was an enormous brass belt buckle, which seemed to symbolize the man's four-square materialistic solidity.

Emerson, on the other hand, had a handsome face with a strong jaw, thick eyebrows, long and well drawn like gulls' wings, and dark, sensitive eyes, more close-set than they should have been, somewhat diminishing an otherwise intelligent aspect.

Leonard commenced pacing the room, his arms folded across his chest, while Emerson remained seated at his desk. Behind him was a wallscreen covered with schematic displays of troop deployment.

"Perhaps Rudolph's plan," Leonard mused.

"I strongly oppose it, Comman—"

"You're too cautious, Emerson," Leonard interrupted. "Too cautious for your own good."

"We had no choice, Commander. Our losses—"

"Don't talk to me of *losses*, man! We can't let these aliens run roughshod over us! I propose we adopt Rudolph's strategy. A surgical strike is our only recourse."

Emerson thought about objecting, but Leonard had swung around and slammed his hands flat on the table, silencing him almost before he began.

"I will not tolerate any delays!" the commander warned him, bulldog jowls shaking. "If Rudolph's plan doesn't meet with your approval, then come up with a better one!"

Emerson stifled a retort and averted his eyes. For an

instant, the commander's shaved head inches from his own, he understood why Leonard was known to some as Little Dolza.

"Certainly, Commander," he said obediently. "I understand." What Emerson understood was that Chairman Moran and the rest of the UEG council were beginning to question Leonard's fitness to command, and Leonard was feeling the screws turn.

Leonard's cold gaze remained in place. "Good," he said, certain he had made himself clear. "Because I want an end to all this madness and I'm holding *you* responsible. . . . After all," he added, turning and walking away, "you're supposed to be the miracle man."

The 15th had a clear view of the jagged ridgeline and downed fortress from their twelfth-story quarters in the barracks compound. Between the compound and twin peaks that dominated the view, the land was lifeless and incurably rugged, cratered from the countless Zentraedi death bolts rained upon it almost twenty years before.

The barracks ready-room was posh by any current standards: spacious, well-lit, equipped with features more befitting a recreation room, including video games and a bar. Most of the squad was done in, already in the sack or on their way, save for Dana Sterling, too wired for sleep, Angelo Dante, who had little use for it on any occasion, and Sean Phillips, who was more than accustomed to long hours.

The sergeant couldn't tear himself away from the view, and seemed itching to get back into battle.

"We should still be out there fighting—am I right or am I right?" Angelo pronounced, directing his words to

Sean only because he was seated nearby. "We'll be fighting this war when our pensions come due unless we defeat those monsters with one big shot; the whistle blows and everybody goes."

At twenty-six, the sergeant was the oldest member of the 15th, also the tallest, loudest, and deadliest—as sergeants are wont to be. He had met his match for impulsiveness in Dana, and recklessness in Sean, but the final results had yet to be tallied.

Sean, chin resting on his hand, had his back turned to the windows and to Angie. Long-haired would-be Casanova of the 15th and of nearly every other outfit in the barracks compound, he fancied conquests of a softer sort. But at the moment he was too exhausted for campaigns of any class.

"The brass'll figure out what to do, Angie," he told the sergeant tiredly, still regarding himself as a lieutenant no matter what the brass thought of him. "Haven't you heard? They know everything. Personally, I'm tired."

Angelo stopped pacing, looking around to make sure Bowie wasn't there. "By the way, what's with Bowie?"

This seemed to bring Sean around some, but Angelo declined to follow his comment up with an explanation.

"Why? He got a problem? You should have said something during the debriefing."

The sergeant put his hands on this hips. "He's been screwing up. That's not a *problem* in combat; it's a major malfunction."

Some would have expected the presence of the fortress to have cast a pall over the city, but that was not the case. In fact, in scarcely a week's time the often silent ship (except when stirred up by the armies of the Southern Cross) had become an accepted feature of the landscape, and something of an object of fascination. Had the area of the crash site not been cordoned off, it's likely that half of Monument would have streamed up into the hills in hopes of catching a glimpse of the thing. As it was, business went on as usual. But historians and commentators were quick to offer explanations, pointing to the behavior of the populace of besieged cities of the past, Beirut of the last century, and countless others during the Global Civil War at the century's end.

Even Dana Sterling, and Nova Satori, the cool but alluring lieutenant with the Global Military Police, were not immune to the fortress's ominous enchantment. Even though they had both seen the deadlier side of its nature revealed.

Just now they shared a table in one of Monument's most popular cafés—a checkerboard-patterned tile floor, round tables of oak, and chairs of wrought iron—with a view of the fortress that surpassed the barracks' overlook.

Theirs had been less than a trouble-free relationship, but Dana had made a deal with herself to try to patch things up. Nova was agreeable and had an hour or so she could spare.

They were in their uniforms, their techno-hairbands in place, and as such the two women looked like a pair of military bookends: Dana, short and lithe, with a globe of swirling blond hair; and taller Nova, with her polished face and thick fall of black hair.

But they were hardly of a mind about things.

"I have lots of dreams," Dana was saying, "the waking kind and the sleeping kind. Sometimes I dream about meeting a man and flying to the edge of the universe with him—"

She caught herself abruptly. How in the world had she gotten onto this subject? She had started of by apologizing, explaining the pressures she had been under. Then somehow she had considered confiding to Nova about the disturbing images and trances concerning the red Bioroid pilot, the one called Zor, not certain whether the MP lieutenant would feel duty-bound to report the matter.

Maybe it had something to do with looking at the fortress and knowing the red Bioroid was out there somewhere? And then all of a sudden she was babbling about her childhood fantasies and Nova was studying her with a get-the-straitjacket look.

"Don't you think it's time you grew up?" said Nova. "Took life a little more seriously?"

Dana turned to her, the spell broken. "Listen, I'm as attentive to duty as the next person! I didn't get my commission just because of who my parents are, so don't patronize me—huh?"

She jumped to her feet. A big MP had just come in with Bowie, looking hangdog, traipsing behind. The MP saluted Nova and explained.

"We caught him in an off-limits joint, ma'am. He has a valid pass, but what shall we do with him?"

"Not a word, Dana!" Nova cautioned. Then she asked the MP, "Which off-limits place?"

"A bar over in the Gauntlet, ma'am."

"Wait a minute," said Bowie, hoping to save his neck. "It wasn't a bar, ma'am, it was a jazz club!" He looked back and forth between Nova and Dana, searching for the line of least resistance, realizing all the while that it was a fine line between bar and club. But being busted for drinking was going to cost him more points than straying into a restricted area. Maybe if he displayed the guilt they obviously expected him to feel . . .

"Where they have been known to roll soldiers who wake up bleeding in some alley!" Nova snapped. "If the army didn't need every ATAC right now, I'd let you think that over for a week in the lockup!"

Nova was forcing the harsh tone in her voice. What she actually felt was closer to amusement than anger. Any minute now Dana would try to intervene on Grant's behalf; and Grant was bound to foul up again, which would then reflect on Dana. Nova smiled inside: it felt so good to have the upper hand.

Bowie was stammering an explanation and apology, far from heartfelt, but somehow convincing. Nova, however, put a quick end to it and continued to read him the riot act.

"And furthermore, I fully appreciate the pressure you've all been under, but we can't afford to make allowances for *special cases*. Do you understand me, *Private*?!"

The implication was clear enough: Bowie was being warned that his relationship with General Emerson wouldn't be taken into account.

Dana was gazing coldly at Bowie, nodding along with the lieutenant's lecture, but at the same time she was managing to slip Bowie a knowing wink, as if to say: *Just agree with her.*

Bowie caught on at last. "I promise not to do it again, *sir*!"

Meanwhile Nova had turned to Dana. "If Lieutenant Sterling is willing to take responsibility for you and keep you out of trouble, I'll let this incident go. But next time I won't be so lenient."

Dana consented, her tone suggesting rough things ahead for Bowie Grant, and Nova dismissed her agent.

"Shall we finish our coffee?" Nova asked leadingly.

Dana thought carefully before responding. Nova was up to no good, but Dana suddenly saw a way to turn the incident to her own advantage. And Bowie's as well.

"I think it would be better if I started *proving* myself to you by taking care of my new responsibility," she said stiffly.

"Yes, you do that," Nova drawled, sounding like the Wicked Witch of the West.

Later, walking back to the barracks, Dana had some serious words with her charge.

"Nova's not playing around. Next time she'll probably feed you to the piranhas. Bowie, what's wrong? First you louse up in combat, then you go looking for trouble in town. And where'd you steal a valid pass, by the way?"

He shrugged, head hung. "I keep spares. Sorry, I didn't mean to cause any friction between you and Nova. You're a good friend, Dana."

Dana smiled down at him. "Okay . . . but there's one thing you can do for me . . ."

Bowie was waiting for her to finish, when Dana's open hand came around without warning and slapped him forcefully on the back—almost throwing him off his feet —and with it Dana's hearty: "Cheer up! Everything's going to be fine!"

ABOUT THE AUTHOR

Jack McKinney has been a psychiatric aide, fusion-rock guitarist and session man, worldwide wilderness guide, and "consultant" to the U.S. Military in Southeast Asia (although they had to draft him for that).

His numerous other works of mainstream and science fiction—novels, radio and television scripts—have been written under various pseudonyms.

He currently resides in Dos Lagunas, El Petén, Guatemala.